# CYPRESS TOMBS

Shane Lege

**Check out my other great books at:**
https://shanelege.com
Or by scanning the QR code below

TikTok: @shanelege
Twitter: @ShaneLege
Instagram: LegeIndustriesLLC
Facebook: Lege Industries LLC
Good Reads: Shane Lege

ISBN- 978-1-961387-45-4

## *Chapter 1*

Leah Broussard often wondered how she would die, especially in a town like Gueydan, where life was quiet, predictable, and traditional. The bayou made you think about things like that—about how time would eventually catch up with everyone. But no matter how much her mind had wandered down that path, she never imagined her life would end like this.

Her wrists were bound tightly behind her back, the coarse rope biting into her skin. A blindfold pressed against her eyes, thick enough to block out every hint of light. She could feel the gag in her mouth, rough fabric cutting into the corners of her lips, silencing any cry she might have had the strength to make. The air around her was heavy with the scent of damp earth and decay, unfamiliar and foreign, leaving her disoriented and uncertain. Wherever she was, it wasn't Gueydan—it wasn't anywhere she recognized.

Leah's heart raced, her chest rising and falling in quick, shallow breaths. She knew she was in trouble. There was no denying the fear that gnawed at her insides, the terrifying possibility that this could be the end. She could feel her muscles tense with every futile attempt to struggle free, panic beginning to flood her senses. She had no idea how she had ended up here, in this dark, godforsaken place, but whoever had taken her wasn't about to let her go.

Yet amid the terror, there was something else. Something that crawled up from deep within her, stirring where she least expected it. A strange thrill coursed through her veins, a part of her body reacting to the danger and helplessness. It confused her—how could she be

1

afraid for her life and yet, somewhere in the depths of her mind, feel a twisted sense of excitement? The sensation gripped her in ways she didn't fully understand, a dark current pulling her under as she desperately tried to stay afloat.

Part of her was scared to death, every instinct screaming at her to find a way out, to escape before it was too late. But another small, forbidden part of her was turned on by the situation—the powerlessness, the unknown. It was the kind of thing she had never spoken of, not even to herself, but now it was undeniable. The boundaries between fear and desire blurred, and for a fleeting moment, she wasn't sure which one was stronger.

Was it the adrenaline? The overwhelming sense of being at someone else's mercy? Or maybe it was the thought that in losing control, she had tapped into something deeper, something primal that lived in the shadows of her soul. Whatever it was, it scared her almost as much as the danger she was in.

Leah's thoughts drifted back to the days leading up to this nightmare, replaying them repeatedly, hoping to find some clue she had missed. Was there something that should've stood out? A strange glance from a stranger, a fleeting conversation that felt off, or an unsettling gut feeling she had brushed aside? Each moment felt hazy now, as if she were trying to remember a dream that was slipping away. She tried to piece together her memories, but they felt like fragments of a puzzle with too many pieces missing, each one more elusive than the last. The harder she tried to make sense of it, the more distant it seemed.

Leah wasn't a supermodel, but her beauty was undeniable. At thirty-six years old, she carried herself with the confidence and grace from experience. Softened by motherhood, her figure was still attractive, her body's natural curves a testament to her life. She had two children, and while her body had changed with time, she remained striking in a way beyond physical appearance.

Her curly blonde hair, often untamed and full of life, framed her face perfectly, accentuating her warm, inviting features. She stood at around five feet four inches, her petite stature balanced by an inner strength that everyone who knew her could sense. Her eyes, a deep, mesmerizing shade of blue, were her most captivating feature. They were the kind of eyes that drew people in, eyes that could make someone feel seen, understood, and cared for. It was easy to get lost in them as if they held stories untold, depths uncharted.

Leah seemed to connect with others naturally. Her personality was magnetic, and her laughter was infectious. People were drawn to her not just because of her beauty but also because of her warmth and kindness. She was fun to be around, always bringing lightness and joy to those in her presence. Leah had a gift for making people feel comfortable like they belonged, and she took pride in supporting her friends and family, always encouraging them to chase their dreams and passions.

She wasn't the type to harbor ill will or speak negatively of others. Her heart was as generous as her smile, and her spirit was uplifting. Whether through a kind word, a shared laugh, or simply being there when needed, Leah had a way of brightening the lives of those around her. She was, in every sense, the kind of person people loved to have in their corner—loyal, compassionate, and effortlessly charming.

Her last clear memory before everything went wrong was of the Duck Festival in Gueydan, Louisiana. She had attended it every year for the past twenty years, and this year had felt no different—or so she thought at the time. It was a ritual for the people of Gueydan and the surrounding parishes, a weekend of celebration that marked the end of summer, when the humidity clung to the skin and the air buzzed with excitement.

The festival was as predictable as the bayou itself, a comforting routine Leah had grown up with. People came from all over to see one another, to laugh, drink, and share stories over heaping plates of Cajun cuisine. The air was filled with the rich, savory aroma of boudin, jambalaya, and étouffée, blending with the scent of the swamp lingering in the background. It was the kind of place where the line between friend and family blurred, where neighbors were as close as kin. Gueydan wasn't big, but during the Duck Festival, the town swelled with people, their chatter filling the streets like the hum of cicadas in summer.

Amidst the noise of laughter and lively conversations, the familiar strains of Jesse Lege's voice echoed from the festival stage. He was singing "Jole Blon," the haunting Cajun waltz that always tugged at her heart. Leah remembered standing there, listening to the song, the music blending with the clink of beer bottles and the clamor of children running through the crowd. The lyrics were bittersweet, and as she heard them, she felt a pang of nostalgia—though she couldn't place why. Maybe it was the song, seeing the same faces year after year, or perhaps something more profound, a suspicion she hadn't recognized at the time.

She remembered scanning the crowd, looking at all the familiar faces, the same people who had been coming to this festival for decades. Everyone seemed at ease, caught up in the joy of the moment. But as she replayed those scenes in her mind, Leah couldn't help but wonder—was someone there who didn't belong? A stranger whose face she didn't recognize, whose presence felt wrong? Had someone been watching her from the crowd's edges, someone she had brushed off as another festival-goer? Or maybe it had been something subtler—a glance that lingered too long, a conversation with an uneasy undercurrent she hadn't noticed.

Could the abductor also be from the small town of Gueydan, where life moved slowly? Nestled deep in the bayous, it was the place where everyone knew everyone, and you could walk down the street waving at familiar faces without worrying about a thing. The town sat about 20-something miles south of Interstate 10 in Vermillion Parish, a forgotten stretch of highway where folks from out of town rarely ventured unless they had a good reason. Gueydan wasn't a place people just stumbled upon—it was more like a secret you had to be told about.

Days in Gueydan were passed by in a rhythm as predictable as the ebb and flow of the nearby marshes. Mornings began with the soft hum of cicadas, the air thick with humidity, and the scent of the bayou drifting through the wind. As the sun climbed higher in the sky, life slowed even more. It was the quiet that felt like it could go on forever, where nothing out of the ordinary ever happened.

Gueydan was a town with deep roots, where tradition and nature intertwined. Known as the "Duck Capital of the World," it earned that title from the vast marshlands stretching like a blanket of green and gold. The marshes were a haven for wildlife, teeming with ducks, geese, and fish, drawing hunters and anglers from miles away. Every year, during duck season, the town would be filled with outdoor people looking to experience the untouched wilderness surrounding it. Unlike many other places, modern development left Gueydan's landscape relatively unspoiled. The marshes remained as wild as they had been for centuries, offering a glimpse into a world few had access to.

But Gueydan itself wasn't just a desLeahtion for hunters. It was a small, close-knit town with a population that had remained mostly unchanged for generations. It was where family names carried weight, and people could trace their lineage to the early settlers who had carved out a life in the bayous. In Gueydan, everyone knew everyone. You couldn't walk down the street without stopping to chat with someone, whether you wanted to or not. Life there moved slowly, but it was alive with the sound of people's voices, their conversations carrying on the wind.

In a town this small, privacy was almost nonexistent. Everyone knew each other's business; if they didn't, they acted like they did. Rumors spread faster than wildfire on a dry summer day, with bits of gossip jumping from person to person, often growing and changing with each retelling. When a story went through town, it was less about what happened and more about what people wanted to believe. If a marriage broke up or someone's business struggled, the whole town would know before the day ended. Even the most minor event fueled the rumor mill, each person adding flair to the story until it became almost unrecognizable.

Gueydan wasn't the kind of place where big corporations found a foothold. No chain stores or fast-food restaurants were lining the streets. The only recognizable brands were the gas stations where locals and visitors filled up before heading out into the marshes. Everything else was locally owned, and small businesses were passed down through generations. Mom-and-pop shops dominated Main Street—places like the family-owned grocery store, the bait shop selling everything from live worms to hunting licenses, and the local diner, where everyone gathered for a plate of biscuits and gravy and a conversation.

The people who ran these businesses were the backbone of the town. They had grown up in Gueydan, gone to school there, and likely never left. Many had taken over from their parents, continuing the family legacy with little thought of leaving for bigger cities or different lives. They were a part of the town's fabric, just like the marshes were a part of the land. In Gueydan, change came slowly, if at all. Life was predictable and steady, and everyone seemed to prefer it that way.

But that sense of stability also came with a downside. The same close-knit community that made people feel connected could also feel stifling. Everyone knew where you came from, what you did for a living, and who your parents were. If something went wrong, you couldn't hide it—no matter how hard you tried. Secrets were hard to keep in a town like Gueydan. If something unusual happened, like a stranger coming to town or an unexpected scandal, the entire community buzzed with speculation, dissecting every detail until nothing was left to discuss.

Everything led right back to the Duck Festival. For a town as small and tight-knit as Gueydan, the festival was one of the few times when the usual boundaries blurred, and unfamiliar faces could slip in without causing too much of a stir. If strangers had come into town any other time, they would've stuck out like a sore thumb. In Gueydan, new faces were rare, and it didn't take long for people to notice when someone new showed up. The town had a way of keeping track of its own—the residents mentally cataloged every person, every car, every unfamiliar movement.

Usually, when someone new arrived in town, the gossip train kicked into high gear. People would whisper about who the stranger might be, where they came from, and their business in Gueydan. Speculation ran wild—especially if the person didn't seem to fit. Was it a hunter passing through, or maybe a distant relative visiting family? No matter how innocuous the reason for their presence, everyone in town would know within hours. It was just the way things worked. Strangers couldn't go unnoticed for long, not in a place like Gueydan.

But the Duck Festival was different. It was the one time of year when the town opened its arms to the outside world, welcoming people from surrounding areas and even further afield. Hunters, tourists, and festival-goers flooded in, swelling the town beyond its usual size. The typically quiet streets became packed with cars, and the crowd grew to include unfamiliar faces—people who hadn't grown up in Gueydan, who didn't know its history or people.

During the festival, the usual social radar was overwhelmed. Locals were too busy enjoying the festivities to keep track of every new person who passed through. The music, the food, and the laughter created a haze of celebration that allowed strangers to blend into the crowd. For once, people weren't paying attention to who was from town and who wasn't. There was no gossip about outsiders because no one kept tabs on them. The festival was a break from the usual routine when the small-town bubble expanded, if only for a few days.

That's why, in Leah's mind, everything circled back to the Duck Festival. If someone had wanted to slip into Gueydan unnoticed, the festival would've been the perfect cover. It was the only time a stranger could move through town without drawing attention, their presence hidden among the crowds of out-of-towers. No one would think twice about a new face during the festival—they'd assume the person was another visitor, there to enjoy the music and Cajun cuisine.

The more Leah thought about it, the more it made sense. If her abductor had been someone from outside Gueydan, the festival would have been the moment they arrived. The question was, why? Why come to Gueydan? Why target her? And how had they managed to pull off the abduction without anyone noticing?

It gnawed at her, the idea that someone had been watching her, planning this while everyone else was too distracted by the festival to notice. It would explain why there hadn't been any whispers of a stranger in town before the Duck Festival. If someone had been laying the groundwork, they had done so during the only time they could blend in without raising suspicion.

Leah couldn't shake the feeling that everything had been set in motion during those few chaotic days. The festival had been the perfect smokescreen, and whoever had taken her knew it. They had used the anonymity of the event to get close, to study her without tipping anyone off. The festival, which had always been a source of joy and celebration, had now become the moment when her life began to unravel.

However, the festival had felt so ordinary, but now, looking back, Leah wondered if it had been anything but. What had seemed like an ordinary evening of music, food, and laughter had ended with her abduction. That thought alone sent a chill through her. She couldn't shake the feeling that she had missed something crucial, something small but significant. But what was it? What had she overlooked?

The pieces of her memory were scattered; no matter how hard she tried to fit them together, they wouldn't form a clear picture. The last thing she recalled was Jesse Lege's voice fading as she walked away from the festival grounds, her feet kicking up dust from the dry Louisiana dirt. Everything after that was a blur—until she woke up bound and helpless, her world turned upside down.

She couldn't help but wonder if the festival had been the beginning of it all. Had someone been watching her that night, waiting for the perfect moment to strike? Or was it all just coincidence, and the real danger lurked elsewhere, waiting to drag her into the darkness when she least expected it?

## Chapter 2

As Chris and Johnny stepped out of their trucks into the early morning darkness, Chris shivered and remarked, "Man, it's freezing out here this morning."

"I know," Johnny replied, rubbing his hands together. "It's so cold I can barely feel my fingers. I made sure to wear the thick gloves today."

Chris glanced up at the overcast sky as they began preparing their shotguns and gear for the hunt. "Wouldn't think it'd be this cold with all these clouds overhead," he noted.

Johnny nodded, shutting his truck door with a thud. "Right? Hopefully, the ducks are flying low this morning because of the cloud cover."

"Yeah, let's hope so," Chris agreed as he walked around the front of his truck to join Johnny. "I've been waiting all week to get out here and put some ducks in the freezer."

Johnny glanced at the dim horizon and said, "Well, let's get down to the bayou before daylight hits. Those ducks aren't going to come to us out here in the open next to the trucks."

"Agreed," Chris responded as he let the hunting dogs out of the back of the truck. "Let's head down the levee next to the canal to get back there."

For about 25 years, Chris Cormier and Johnny Fontenot had made hunting along the bayou a tradition that anchored their friendship and love for the outdoors. Every weekend during duck season, the two men could be found trudging through the marshes, shotguns slung over their shoulders and gear packed for the day ahead. The bayou, with its twisting waterways and dense reeds, was like a second home to them—a place where they could escape the demands of everyday life and immerse themselves in nature's quiet, untamed beauty.

Johnny and Chris were both born and raised in Gueydan, Louisiana, where they went to school together, played football, and often got into trouble as kids. Now in their late thirties, they still looked young enough to pass for their early thirties.

Johnny stood around six feet tall, with brown hair, blue eyes, and a lean frame. Chris, slightly shorter than Johnny, had black hair, brown eyes, a beard, and a more athletic build. Both men deeply loved the area, which they considered a true Sportsman's Paradise, offering year-round opportunities for hunting and fishing.

Rarely did they miss a weekend during the season. Duck hunting wasn't just a hobby for Chris and Johnny but a passion. It allowed them to reconnect after the busy workweek, sharing stories, trading jokes, and talking about life. Something about the stillness of the early mornings, the soft lapping of water against the banks, and the rustle of the wind through the trees made these moments feel special. The excitement of the hunt was part of it—the thrill of watching ducks soar low over the marsh, taking aim, and hearing the echo of their shots reverberate across the water. But more than that, their bond strengthened over the years of these early morning outings.

The family was always a priority for both men. They spent their weekdays working hard, providing for their loved ones, and making time for their wives and children. But when duck season rolled around, they always found a way to sneak off to the bayou. Their families understood—it was part of who they were. Their wives joked that the men had "duck fever," something that couldn't be cured, only temporarily relieved by weekends spent in the marsh. Chris and Johnny would laugh and nod, knowing it was true.

Hunting along the bayou had become more than just a pastime—it was tradition, a ritual that had woven itself into the fabric of their lives. They had been doing it so long that the movements were instinctual now: the way they loaded their trucks in the predawn hours, their silent trek to the water's edge, the familiar rhythm of their conversation as they waited for the first ducks to appear. They rarely needed words to communicate when they were out there—years of hunting together had given them an unspoken understanding. A nod, a glance, or a quick gesture was all it took.

Each hunting season, they carried with them memories of years past. Some days, they returned home with coolers full of ducks; other times, they returned empty-handed. But the hunt was never just about the kill. It was about the experience—the camaraderie, the peace of the bayou, and the satisfaction of knowing they were part of something bigger, something timeless. Week after week, year after year, they returned to the bayou to hunt and reconnect—with nature, each other, and themselves.

As they made their way down the familiar levee, the early morning light barely breaking through the thick clouds, Johnny couldn't help but chuckle at an old memory. With its uneven path alongside the canal, the levee was the same place where they had walked countless times before. But this particular memory stood out more than most.

"Chris, do you remember when we walked down this same levee and heard something running toward us purposefully?" Johnny asked, the amusement evident in his voice.

Chris grinned, the recollection coming back to him instantly. "Yup," he replied, continuing to walk beside Johnny. "We thought it was that black panther everyone used to talk about, the one that prowled the area. It sure sounded like it was coming straight for us."

Johnny's laugh grew louder. "Yeah, and we cocked our shotguns, thinking we were about to face off with a panther. We were so sure we would have to fight for our lives!"

Chris couldn't help but chuckle, shaking his head at the memory. "Until we got a good look at what was coming our way," he said, grinning. "It was just one of my hunting dogs, bounding toward us like it was the happiest thing in the world. Nearly scared us half to death for nothing. I think I almost peed myself that day."

Johnny burst out laughing, nearly doubling over as the memory flooded back. "Me too!" he said between laughs. "We were so worked up, thinking we would have to take down a black panther, and it was just your dog! I swear, I've never been that relieved and embarrassed simultaneously."

The two men continued walking, their laughter echoing across the quiet marsh. The stillness of the bayou contrasted with their lighthearted conversation, the distant calls of ducks the only other sound in the cool air.

"I wonder whatever happened to that old panther," Chris said after the laughter died. He looked out over the water as if the creature might suddenly reappear after all these years.

"I don't know," Johnny replied, his tone thoughtful now. "I haven't heard anyone mention seeing her in a while. It's like she just disappeared."

"Funny thing is," Chris said, "whenever anyone spotted her, none of us ever had a gun on us. We'd always be unarmed, just watching her slink away into the brush. She knew we weren't a threat when we weren't carrying."

"Yeah," Johnny mused, "I wonder why that was. Every time someone saw her, we were all standing there, not even a shotgun in sight."

Chris shrugged, a hint of mystery lingering in his voice. "No one knows. It was just one of those things that always happened when we least expected it."

They fell into a comfortable silence for a few moments; both men lost in thought, their boots crunching along the dirt of the levee. The memory of the panther—and the absurdity of that day—stirred something nostalgic in both of them.

"You know," Johnny said, breaking the silence with a smile, "some stories get old after a while, but not that one. I feel like we'll be talking about it until the day we die."

Chris chuckled softly and nodded in agreement, the memory of that day as vivid as if it had just happened. "You're probably right. That was over twenty years ago; we still discuss it like yesterday. Some things stick with you, especially out here. Like when we were all standing on the levee by the trucks."

Johnny's grin widened as he recalled the moment. "Oh yeah, and something jumped into the water behind us."

Chris shook his head in disbelief, even after all these years. "Yep, and all four of us spun around and unloaded our shotguns into the water without thinking twice. No idea what was there—just pure instinct."

Johnny laughed, its absurdity still making him shake his head. "We still have no clue what it was. It could've been a fish, an alligator, or even a snake. We'll never know."

They both paused momentarily, remembering the adrenaline and the way the marsh had fallen eerily silent after the echo of their gunshots had faded into the mist.

"The only thing we knew for sure," Chris continued, a smirk creeping onto his face, "was that whatever it was, it wasn't living after that. We made sure of that."

After about fifteen to twenty minutes of walking, Chris and Johnny reached the edge of Bayou Queue De Tortue, a spot that felt more like home than almost anywhere else. The bayou, with its winding waterways, towering cypress trees, and thick brush, was a place they had spent countless hours exploring, hunting, and even just sitting in quiet reflection. Over the years, they had become so familiar with it that every step felt instinctual as if the land had become part of their muscle memory.

They rarely needed much light to guide them through the early morning darkness. They could easily find their way, even under the faint glow of dawn or with nothing but the moon to light their path. They knew precisely where the tall, gnarled trees stood, where the ancient cypress stumps jutted out from the earth, and where every dip and rise in the ground could be found. Every curve of the bayou, every ripple in the water—they knew it all by heart. There was comfort in that familiarity, in understanding the land so well that they could move through it almost blindfolded.

Chris always veered off to the left, guiding the dogs along the familiar stretch of the bayou, while Johnny instinctively headed to the right. It was a routine they had perfected over years of hunting together that required no discussion. Their movements had a natural rhythm—an unspoken understanding built over countless early mornings in the marsh. They both knew their paths by heart, the steps as familiar as breathing. Without a word exchanged, they split off, heading toward their respective blinds.

The bayou was still dark, the early morning mist hanging low over the water, swirling in the cold air. Their boots crunched softly against the damp earth as they moved, the silence of the marsh broken only by the occasional splash from the dogs or the faint rustle of the wind through the trees. The world felt muted in those moments before dawn, as if the bayou was holding its breath, waiting for the first light of day.

Chris and Johnny reached their duck blinds, simple structures they had built and rebuilt over the years, hidden well enough to blend into the natural surroundings. Once settled, neither man spoke. There was no need. Both of them were focused on the same thing—waiting for the official break of daylight.

They both stared out along the bayou, taking in the beauty of nature. It was not entirely daylight yet, but enough light that the cypress stumps along the edges of the bayou had a rugged, almost ancient appearance, weathered by time and the elements. Their broad, gnarled bases rose out of the dark, murky water like the twisted roots of a forgotten forest, their bark rough and textured with deep ridges. Some stumps were hollowed out, worn down by years of exposure to the elements, while others stood stout and solid, their wood dark and dense, hints of moss clinging to their surfaces.

The cypress knees, smaller stumps that jutted up like eerie fingers, surrounded the larger trunks, creating a jagged, natural barrier along the water's edge. Their strange, knobby shapes seemed to twist and curl out of the bayou, some standing tall like ancient sentinels while others barely skimmed the water's surface, hidden beneath the dense greenery.

The stumps themselves were bleached in places, the wood sun-bleached to a pale, silvery gray where it protruded from the water, while their lower portions remained darker, slick with the bayou's moisture. In some spots, algae and thick patches of moss gave the stumps a greenish hue, blending them into the surrounding marsh. Vines wound around some of the older stumps while ferns and other plants grew from their cracks, giving them the look of something that nature had reclaimed.

As the first light of dawn crept across the horizon, casting a soft glow over the bayou, Chris raised his duck call to his lips. The air was still thick with anticipation, and he could feel the familiar surge of excitement as he blew into the call, the sound echoing across the marsh. It was a practiced rhythm he had honed over years of hunting, mimicking the calls of the ducks he had spent so many mornings tracking. After each call, Chris paused, his eyes scanning the sky, waiting to hear that telltale response.

The silence that followed stretched on, broken only by the subtle rustle of the wind through the trees and the occasional splash from the water. He blew into the call again, this time more forcefully, his breath producing a low, resonant sound that drifted out over the water. He waited again, his pulse steady, his body perfectly still in the blind. Chris had learned the art of patience out here—knowing that sometimes it took time to coax the ducks from the sky.

Minutes passed, and just as he was about to call again, he heard a faint quack in the distance. His heart leaped at the sound. The duck was answering somewhere off to his left, and he could hear the flap of wings as it drew nearer. Quickly but quietly, he shifted his position, raising his shotgun and readying himself. He had done this countless times before, but each hunt carried its thrill, its moment of suspended time before the action began.

The duck was coming in fast now; its wing beats slicing through the air. Chris's eyes followed the sound, scanning the sky for that first glimpse. He knew it wouldn't be long before the bird came into view. Every muscle in his body tensed with focus, his finger resting lightly on the trigger, waiting for the right moment.

And then, there it was—a flash of movement against the early morning light. The duck flew into view, skimming low over the water, right where Chris had anticipated. Without hesitation, he aimed, his shotgun tracking the duck's flight path, and pulled the trigger. The sharp crack of the shot echoed through the bayou, followed by the quiet splash as the duck hit the water.

Chris immediately released the dogs, and in an instant, they darted out of the duck blind with practiced precision. Their paws pounded against the wet, marshy ground, the rapid thud of their footsteps mingling with the soft rustling of the reeds. The early morning quiet was suddenly interrupted by a splash as they leaped into the bayou, sending ripples through the still water. Chris watched closely, his eyes trained on their sleek forms as they swam with purpose toward the downed duck. The bayou, so familiar to them, had become their playground, and they navigated it effortlessly.

The dogs reached the spot where the duck had fallen, their heads bobbing above the water as they expertly retrieved it. Chris stood in the duck blind, already anticipating their swift return. Typically, the dogs were as reliable as the sunrise—quick to retrieve, quick to bring the game back. They'd done this a hundred times before, and Chris trusted them completely. He could already picture them trotting back through the marsh, the duck in their jaws, ready for the next round.

But something was different this time.

Instead of swimming straight back to shore, the dogs hesitated, their bodies tensing as they reached the bank. Chris furrowed his brow, watching as they paused, still holding the duck but not making their usual direct path toward him. Their heads turned in unison toward a distant point in the marsh; ears perked as if something unseen had caught their attention.

Then came the barking.

At first, it was just one of the dogs—sharp, insistent barks echoing through the bayou. Then the second dog joined in, their voices blending into a chorus of warning. They weren't returning to the duck blind; instead, they stood in the water, barking toward something out of sight, their bodies tense with alertness.

Chris's heart quickened. This wasn't normal behavior. He squinted into the distance, trying to see what had drawn their attention, but the thick morning mist and the dense marshland made it impossible to see what they were reacting to. His grip tightened on his shotgun, his instincts kicking in. The dogs weren't barking at the duck but at something else, they perceived as a threat.

Johnny glanced over, concerned. "What's going on with the dogs?"

"I'm not sure," Chris replied, squinting into the distance. "I can't see anything from here."

"We should probably quiet them down before they scare off all the remaining ducks," Johnny suggested.

Chris nodded and called out, "Beau, Luke, come!"

However, the dogs didn't come when called. Instead, they stood firm at the water's edge, barking incessantly, their heads fixed on something neither Johnny nor Chris could see. The sound of their barking echoed across the bayou, unsettling in its intensity. This was entirely out of character for the dogs. Chris had never seen them behave this way in all the years they had been hunting. They were well-trained, disciplined, and always responsive to commands, especially when called back from a retrieval. Yet, today, something had caught their attention so strongly that they ignored him entirely.

"What the hell is out there?" Johnny muttered, his brow furrowed as he scanned the horizon.

Chris shook his head, his grip tightening on his shotgun. "I don't know, but it's not normal. They've never acted like this before."

The dogs' eyes were locked on something in the distance, their bodies tense and alert. The bayou, which had felt peaceful moments before, now seemed ominous. The mist clung to the water's surface, and the trees around them swayed gently in the morning breeze, but everything felt different—like the marsh was holding its breath, waiting for whatever had unsettled the dogs to reveal itself.

Johnny's voice cut through the tension. "You think we need to be worried?"

Chris didn't answer right away. His instincts, honed over years of hunting in the bayou, told him that whatever had captured the dogs' attention wasn't something to take lightly. The dogs had never given them a reason to doubt their judgment, and this time was no different. If they weren't moving or coming back, there was something out there —something neither Chris nor Johnny could see.

"We should check it out," Chris finally said, eyes narrowing as he looked in the direction the dogs were barking. "Whatever it is, they're not going to let up until we know for sure."

Johnny nodded silently, a sense of unease flickering across his face as he moved toward Chris's side. Without exchanging another word, they set off together, their shotguns gripped tightly, ready for whatever awaited. The persistent barking of the dogs led them forward, each step feeling heavier as they ventured deeper into the fog-laden swamp. The thick mist clung to the marsh, stretching as far as they could see, creating an eerie, almost otherworldly atmosphere that blurred the lines between land and water.

As they trudged through the soggy ground, the usual sounds of the bayou seemed muted. The croaking of frogs and the occasional splash of fish breaking the surface were still there, but quieter, as if the bayou sensed something was amiss. Each step squished beneath their boots, the cold dampness of the marsh seeping into the air, making it feel colder than it was.

An unsettling feeling settled deep in their stomachs, a mix of apprehension and curiosity. Chris and Johnny had hunted these lands for years; they knew the swamp inside and out. They had faced their fair share of wildlife—gators, snakes, and everything. But something about this situation felt different. The dogs, usually reliable and calm, were agitated, their barks sharp and insistent. It wasn't a reaction to the game—it was something else neither of them had encountered.

The two men moved cautiously, the weight of the shotguns in their hands comforting but not enough to ease the gnawing tension in the pit of their stomachs. The fog made it difficult to see more than a few yards ahead, and the distant shapes of trees and cypress stumps seemed to shift in the mist, creating an eerie, shifting landscape around them.

"What the hell do you think it is?" Johnny asked in a low voice, his eyes darting around as they approached the dogs.

Chris shook his head, his jaw tight. "I don't know. But the dogs won't stop whatever it is until we figure it out."

The unsettling feeling deepened as they neared the bayou's edge, where the dogs were still barking. Something was out there, hidden in the fog, just beyond their view. The dogs stood stiffly, their bodies tense, still barking furiously at something in the distance, their eyes locked on whatever had captured their attention. This was no ordinary situation—something had spooked them, something neither Chris nor Johnny could see yet.

As they closed in on the spot where the dogs were barking, the fog seemed to part almost unnaturally, revealing the scene that had agitated the dogs so intensely. The thick mist clinging to the bayou lifted just enough, giving Johnny and Chris a clear view of what lay ahead.

At first, their eyes strained to make sense of the shapes before them. But then, the details became clearer—too clear. What they saw stopped them in their tracks. Johnny's stomach turned violently at the sight. His face went pale as he spun around, retching uncontrollably.

Chris, frozen in place, felt the bile rise in his own throat, his mind struggling to process the scene. He forced himself to stay steady, though his heart pounded. The dogs, still barking wildly, circled the water's edge, clearly disturbed by what they had found.

Johnny, his hands on his knees, gasped for air after heaving. "What... what the hell is that?" His voice was barely a whisper, shaking as he spoke.

It wasn't just the shock of what they saw—it was its grotesque, horrific nature. The body of a woman, partially submerged in the murky water, was twisted unnaturally, limbs splayed at odd angles as if something or someone had discarded her there. Her skin, pale and bloated from the water, was barely visible beneath the grime and muck of the swamp. Intermingled among the cypress stumps, it was as if the stumps themselves acted as a grim tomb for the mangled body. The sight was raw, brutal, and utterly unexpected.

## Chapter 3

"We need to get the police," Johnny said, wiping his mouth after vomiting again.

Chris nodded, trying to keep down his rising nausea. The sight of the body had shaken both of them deeply. "Let's head back to the trucks and get help," Johnny suggested.

"We can't both go," Chris countered. "Someone has to stay here and make sure nothing else happens to the body."

"Well, it's not gonna be me," Johnny replied quickly.

"So you're saying I should stay?" Chris asked, raising an eyebrow. "How did I end up drawing the short straw in this imaginary straw draw?"

"Because I've thrown up twice already, and I'm pretty sure a third is coming any second now," Johnny said, glancing nervously at the ground.

Chris hesitated, glancing at the body, then back at Johnny. "What if whoever did this comes back? I don't want to end up like her."

"You've got two dogs and a shotgun," Johnny pointed out, trying to sound convincing.

Chris sighed, still clearly reluctant. "I don't like it, but you're probably right," he muttered, knowing there wasn't much of a choice.

Johnny bolted up the levee, his breath coming in ragged gasps as he pushed himself to reach the trucks. The gruesome image of the body stayed with him, fueling his need to get out of there, but the urge to vomit kept rising in his throat, threatening to overwhelm him again. Every step felt heavier than the last. The trek back seemed endless, far longer than the walk toward the hunting blinds that morning. It was as if the trucks were retreating further into the distance with each stride.

His panic was making him clumsy. Twice already, he had tripped, sprawling face-first into the damp ground. Running in rubber boots, so practical for navigating the soggy marshlands, now seemed like a cruel joke. Heavy and stiff boots dragged at his legs each step, making him lose his balance. He stumbled over uneven patches of earth and exposed roots, the slick mud beneath his feet threatening to send him tumbling again. Each fall jarred his body, leaving scrapes on his hands and knees, but he didn't stop.

Frustration and urgency gnawed at him, but he forced himself back to his feet after every fall. There wasn't time to dwell on the aches or the cuts. His only thought was to get back to the trucks to get help. His legs burned, and his chest ached as he pushed harder, but the bayou's thick fog and winding levee made every step feel like it was dragging him further away from his goal.

With every stumble and fall, Johnny brushed himself off and pressed on, his determination outweighing the exhaustion, the nausea, and the fear that gripped him. He had to get back. Time felt like it was slipping away, and every second spent fumbling in the mud was lost.

Meanwhile, Chris managed to stay composed, though only in a just way. The weight of the situation was pressing down on him, heightened by the oppressive silence of the swamp. Now that Johnny was gone, the isolation felt thicker, more unsettling. The mysteries of the bayou seemed to close in around him. Every creak of a branch, every rustle of leaves in the dense underbrush sent his nerves into overdrive. Each time he heard a noise—a faint twig snap, the flutter of something unseen in the distance—his instincts kicked in, and he'd whip his shotgun in that direction, heart pounding in his chest.

He wasn't just unnerved by the woman's body lying only yards away, though that alone was disturbing enough. What gnawed at him more was the knowledge that someone or something had put her there. He couldn't shake the feeling that whoever did it might still lurk in the shadows, watching him. The bayou, usually so familiar and comforting, now felt foreign and hostile, as if the land had turned against him.

Chris had backed himself and the dogs up to where the levee began, carefully choosing his spot. His survival instincts told him to be ready for anything. He positioned himself with the bayou to his left and open land to his right, ensuring he had a clear view of his surroundings. He knew better than to get trapped between the murky waters of the bayou and the unpredictable swamp. The thought of getting caught in quicksand or a patch of dense marshland with no escape made his skin crawl. The bayou could be as dangerous as any predator if you weren't careful.

His eyes darted back and forth, scanning the landscape for any movement. The dogs, usually calm and obedient, were tense too, their ears perked up and their bodies stiff. They sensed it, too—something was off. Chris swallowed hard, tightening his grip on the shotgun. His mind raced with thoughts of what could happen if whoever had left that body returned. He felt vulnerable and exposed, even with his weapon at the ready. The fog clung to the swamp, wrapping everything in a thick haze that made it difficult to see too far ahead, adding to the suffocating sense of danger.

Every sound seemed magnified in the silence, each moment stretching out longer than the last. The unease settled deep in his bones as he kept his eyes fixed on the surroundings, waiting, listening, and hoping Johnny would get back with help before anything else happened. But in the back of his mind, he knew that out here, in the depths of the bayou, time worked differently, and anything could happen.

The relief of reaching the truck washed over Johnny, but only briefly. His heart still pounded, and his hands trembled as he fumbled with the keys. He wasn't sure if the distance from the woman's body was calming his nerves or the sense of safety the truck offered, but he had no time to linger on that thought. Chris was still out there, alone with that gruesome discovery, and every second counted.

Johnny started the truck and hit the gas, the tires spinning slightly on the gravel road before finding their grip. He drove faster than he should have, the familiar crunch of rocks under the tires drowned out by the engine's roar. His knuckles were white as he gripped the steering wheel, his mind racing as fast as the truck. He knew this road well, but the situation's urgency made every bend in the road feel sharper, every second feel longer.

Dust clouded in his rearview mirror, but he didn't slow down. He knew exactly where he needed to go—Ms. Louisiana Trahan's house was just up the road. She lived alone, but everyone in the area knew she had a phone, and she was one of the few people out in the bayou who did. He had visited her house many times and could probably find it with his eyes closed. That thought gave him a small measure of comfort but didn't ease the growing dread in his chest.

His mind flashed back to Chris, still back at the bayou with that mangled body and whatever threat might still be lurking. Johnny cursed under his breath and pressed harder on the gas pedal. He couldn't shake the fear that if he didn't get to Ms. Trahan's house fast enough, something awful might happen to his best friend. The thought of Chris out there, alone, with no one but the dogs to keep him company, gnawed at Johnny. What if whoever had left that body returned? What if Chris became the next victim?

He pushed those dark thoughts aside, focusing on the road ahead. The sooner he got to Ms. Trahan's house, the sooner he could call for help. His pulse raced with the fear of what might already be happening, and the only thing keeping him from panicking completely was the hope that he'd make it in time. The seemingly endless road stretched before him, but he knew he was close now.

As the trees thinned, Johnny could see the outline of Ms. Trahan's small house through the dust cloud. His heart pounded even harder, but it was from a mix of fear and hope this time. Help was within reach, and he had to get there before it was too late.

Johnny careened into Ms. Trahan's driveway, the truck's tires kicking up dust and gravel as the brakes screeched in protest. The truck stopped, skidding slightly before stopping just inches from her front porch. He didn't think twice about parking even or adequately shutting off the engine. His mind was consumed with one thought: getting to that phone.

In his haste, he flung open the truck door and leaped out, so focused on his mission that he didn't bother closing the door behind him. The keys dangled from the ignition, the engine still running, but none mattered. All that filled his mind was the urgency to call for help. Chris was out there, alone with a dead body, and time was ticking. Johnny sprinted toward Ms. Trahan's front door, his heart pounding in his chest, fueled by fear and adrenaline. Every wasted second felt like an eternity; he couldn't afford to lose more time.

Johnny knocked urgently on Ms. Trahan's door, his voice breathless as he called out, "Ms. Trahan, it's Johnny Fontenot. I need to borrow your phone. It's an emergency."

Ms. Trahan opened the door, her face warm and familiar. "Ma sha, how are you doing this morning?" she asked, unaware of the panic in Johnny's voice.

"Ma'am, I need to use your phone," Johnny replied quickly, trying to stay calm. "We found a woman's body out on the bayou, where we usually go hunting."

Ms. Trahan's eyes widened in shock. "Oh no, that poor woman," she gasped. "You go right ahead. The phone's right over there."

Johnny's hands shook as he grabbed the receiver and dialed a number he knew on Ms. Trahan's ancient rotary phone number. The urgency in his chest clashed with the frustrating slowness of the process. Each number he dialed felt like a marathon—he'd push his finger into the hole, rotate the dial to the right, and then agonizingly wait for it to rewind to its original position before starting the next digit. It was maddeningly slow, each click of the dial echoing in his head like a ticking clock. He seemed to stretch unbearably in time, which already felt like it was slipping away.

Johnny didn't have time to dig through the yellow pages for the Gueydan Police Department's number. Instead, he dialed the number of his friend Michael Fruge, which he knew by heart. Michael was a deputy in the Sheriff's Department and would know exactly what to do. Michael was also familiar with the area, having hunted with Chris and Johnny several times.

Michael answered the phone with a simple "Hello."

Johnny exhaled in relief, grateful Michael had picked up. "Michael, it's Johnny. We need your help. Chris and I found a woman's body out on the Trahan land, near the bayou where we usually hunt."

"You found what?" Michael's voice was filled with disbelief.

"A woman's body," Johnny repeated, louder this time, his urgency clear.

"Is she alive?" Michael asked, his tone shifting to concern.

"I don't think so. The body looked pretty mangled, and there were no signs of life from what we could tell," Johnny replied, fighting the urge to vomit again as the gruesome image flashed in his mind.

"Where exactly did you find the body?" Michael asked, more serious now.

"Just a little way up from Chris's duck blind," Johnny explained. "Chris is still out there to ensure nothing happens to the body."

"Alright, let me grab my gear and make several calls. I'll head that way. Where can I meet you?" Michael asked.

"You'll see our trucks parked by the levee where we usually park when we go hunting," Johnny responded. "Just head down the levee, and we'll meet you there. I've got to get back to Chris to ensure he's alright."

"Got it. See you in a few," Michael said before hanging up.

After notifying someone from the authorities, Johnny leaned forward, placing his hands on his knees, and took a moment to breathe. The weight of the situation hung over him, and though relief flickered at having reached the police, it was overshadowed by the urgency to get back to Chris. He heaved a sigh, straightened himself up, and wiped his brow, knowing he couldn't waste more time.

"Thank you for letting me use your phone, Ms. Trahan," Johnny said, glancing toward her as he prepared to leave. He couldn't shake the anxiety that gnawed at him, but he forced a polite smile.

"You're welcome, Johnny," Ms. Trahan replied warmly, following him to the door. "And tell your momma I said hello!"

Johnny gave her a quick nod, grateful for her help but too distracted to engage. His thoughts were entirely on Chris. He hopped back into his truck, not even bothering to close the door before throwing it into gear. The engine, still running from earlier, growled to life as he backed out of the driveway.

As he pulled away, Ms. Trahan stood on the porch, watching him leave. She waved as Johnny stuck his hand out the window, giving her a quick, almost absentminded wave. His eyes were already on the road ahead, his focus sharpening as he steered back toward the levee.

Dust kicked up behind him as the tires spun on the gravel, the truck bouncing along the uneven road. Johnny wasn't in the same full-blown panic as he had been when rushing to find a phone, but the urgency hadn't entirely left him. His foot pressed harder on the gas than usual, and the dusty trail swirled in the rearview mirror.

Johnny pulled up to the levee where they had parked earlier, his truck stopping slowly as he scanned the area. The vehicles sat just as they had been, but there was no sign of Michael yet. He hadn't expected him to be here already—after all, Michael would have to come from his house, and Johnny had the advantage of heading straight back from Ms. Trahan's. Still, every second felt heavy, the urgency pressing against him like a weight. Without wasting time, Johnny began his trek back down the levee toward the bayou.

As he moved closer, he reminded himself to be cautious. He knew Chris would be on edge, and with their situation, Chris might not wait to identify any movement before pulling the trigger. If Chris heard anything coming from the swamp, he'd likely shoot first and ask questions later. With that in mind, Johnny realized he'd need to start calling out Chris's name well in advance, letting him know he was on his way before he got too close.

Before Johnny could even get his first warning shout-off, the loud blast of a shotgun echoed through the stillness of the bayou. It was sudden, jarring, and sent a cold wave of fear crashing over him. For a split second, Johnny froze, his brain struggling to process what he had just heard. Then, instinct kicked in. Without hesitating, he sprinted toward the direction of the gunfire, his boots pounding against the uneven terrain of the levee.

"Chris! Hold on, I'm coming!" Johnny shouted, his voice strained with urgency and desperation. But he knew, deep down, he was still too far away for Chris to hear him. The swamp stretched out between them, a tangled web of thick trees and marshland, swallowing his voice before it could carry. He cursed under his breath, pushing his legs to move faster. His heart pounded wildly in his chest, not just from the exertion but from the rising panic gnawing at him with every step.

Then, another shotgun blast ripped through the air, louder and closer this time. Johnny's heart raced even faster, his mind spinning in fear. He could feel the weight of dread pressing down on him as he pushed himself to go faster, adrenaline surging through his veins. What was Chris shooting at? His thoughts spiraled with terrifying possibilities. Had the person who left the woman's body come back? Was Chris under attack? Or was something from the bayou—some wild animal, maybe an alligator—threatening him?

Johnny's lungs burned with every breath, the air thick with humidity, making it harder to keep up the pace. But he couldn't stop.

He wouldn't. The image of Chris, along with the body and his shotgun firing into the unknown, filled his mind. The bayou, usually so familiar, had turned into something dark and dangerous, where anything could happen.

"Chris!" Johnny shouted again, louder this time, hoping—praying —that he would hear him this time. His voice cracked with fear, his breath ragged as he pushed himself to run faster, every muscle in his body aching from the strain.

## Chapter 4

"Chris, it's Johnny!" Johnny continued shouting from the levee as he ran, his voice strained with urgency.

Finally, after what felt like an eternity, Chris's voice responded from the distance.

"Johnny, is that you?"

"Yeah, it's me," Johnny called back, still unable to see Chris through the thick fog. "Are you alright? What were you shooting at?"

"I... I'm not sure," Chris replied, his voice shaky. "I heard some strange noises to the east and—I guess I just got spooked."

"Alright, take a deep breath. I'm almost there, so don't shoot when I come down the levee," Johnny reassured him.

Johnny could sense the strain in Chris's voice, the unease from being alone in the swamp for too long. Though it had been less than an hour since Johnny left to make the phone call, it might as well have been an eternity in this environment. The bayou was notorious for playing tricks on the mind—strange sounds, shifting shadows, and the ever-present fog could make the most seasoned hunter feel on edge. Add the creeping thoughts of what they had discovered, and it was no wonder Chris had fired those shots.

As Johnny hurried down the levee, his mind raced with concern for Chris, but he was also acutely aware of the dangers around him. The bayou, with its unpredictable terrain and hidden dangers, had a way of turning a small mistake into a life-threatening situation. Johnny had almost reached the bayou when a sudden sound jolted him from his thoughts. The distinct pounding of hooves—an animal galloping toward him at high speed—broke the stillness.

Johnny's heart jumped into his throat, and for a brief second, his instincts took over. The sound was getting closer, fast, and heavy. His body tensed, adrenaline flooding his system as he realized the danger rushing toward him. Without a second thought, he swung his shotgun from his side, aiming it low toward the ground. Every muscle in his body was ready; his senses heightened to the point where time seemed to slow.

His mind raced through the possibilities—was it a wild boar? An animal from the swamp startled by the gunfire? Or something more sinister? He couldn't afford to take chances. The thick fog rolling through the bayou made it impossible to see clearly, but he could feel the animal closing in, the gallop echoing in his ears, growing louder with each passing second.

Johnny crouched slightly, preparing to shoot if necessary. The swamp sounds—normally so peaceful in their way—now felt oppressive, as if the bayou was watching, waiting. His grip on the shotgun tightened, his finger hovering just above the trigger, ready to react instantly. He didn't have time to think—only to act, and whatever was barreling toward him wouldn't give him much time to figure things out.

Johnny was on high alert, every sense heightened as he waited for whatever was barreling toward him. His finger rested lightly on the trigger, the safety already off, ready to fire at the slightest hint of danger. The thudding of hooves—or paws—grew louder with each passing second, echoing off the trees and bouncing through the fog-filled bayou.

As the shape finally emerged from the haze, Johnny instinctively raised his shotgun, his pulse quickening. He was ready to pull the trigger, but in the split second before he could fire, he recognized the familiar form bounding toward him—one of Chris's dogs. Johnny immediately lowered his weapon, his heart racing but now more from relief than fear.

The dog, oblivious to the tension in the air, wagged its tail as it ran up to greet Johnny, happy and carefree as if the morning had been a typical hunt. Johnny exhaled deeply, letting the tension leave his body. Relief washed over him, not only because the animal wasn't a threat but because he hadn't fired at Chris's dog. The thought of accidentally shooting one of the loyal companions would have weighed heavily on him after everything they'd already been through that day.

He couldn't help but let out a small laugh, a mix of nerves and humor bubbling up. This wasn't the first time one of the dogs had given him a scare on this same levee. His mind flashed back to that earlier hunt years ago when he and Chris had been startled by one of the dogs charging toward them in the fog. It was almost surreal how similar the situation felt, and despite their grim circumstances, Johnny found a brief moment of lightness.

"Well, buddy," Johnny muttered to the dog with a half-smile, "you dogs got a knack for scaring the crap out of me on this levee."

Johnny finally arrived at Chris's location, the dog trotting alongside him. It was clear that Chris wasn't in the best shape, but Johnny could see the relief on his face as he spotted him approaching.

"How are you holding up?" Johnny asked.

"I'm alright, but I'm more than ready to get out of here," Chris replied.

"Yeah, I get that," Johnny said. "I called Michael Fruge—he's on his way from his house, so it shouldn't be much longer."

"Good," Chris said with a sigh. "I'm ready to put all of this behind me."

"Same here," Johnny agreed.

Before they could speak again, a commotion erupted from the direction of the levee. Both men instinctively readied their shotguns, unsure of what was causing the noise. Moments later, they were relieved to hear the familiar voice of Michael Fruge calling out.

"Johnny, Chris, you guys okay?" Michael shouted.

"Yeah, we're fine," Johnny answered.

"What was all that shooting about?" Michael asked.

"Nothing serious," Johnny quickly replied, trying to cover for Chris. "Chris was just trying to scare off some wildlife getting too close to the body."

"Oh, well, that's a bit of a relief," Michael said, sounding more relaxed.

"How did you get here so fast?" Johnny asked, surprised.

"We pulled up right as the gunshots went off," Michael explained. "So we sprinted down here."

"We?" Johnny questioned.

"I radioed for backup, and a couple of deputies were nearby, so they met me at the levee," Michael clarified.

Chris and Johnny could now see Michael and the two deputies coming off the levee. They were both relieved and glad to see them as they walked over to greet them.

The two deputies with Michael were Mark Thibodeaux and Thomas Landry. Chris and Johnny knew them well, as they had all grown up together. Mark and Thomas were a little younger than Chris and Johnny, but it was still a small town where everyone knew everyone.

"Man, are we glad to see you guys," Johnny said with relief.

"Where's the body you mentioned?" Michael asked.

"Over there, mixed in with the cypress knees," Chris replied, pointing toward the area.

"Alright, Mark and I will check it out, and Thomas will take your statements to ensure everything is accurate," Michael explained.

"That's fine, but we'd like to get out of here as soon as possible," Chris said. "I've seen enough today, and I don't want to be around when you start dealing with the body."

"Understandable. Let us take your statements and assess the situation, and you should be free to go," Michael assured him. "We'll contact you with further questions about the case."

"We get it, and we'll help however we can," Johnny said. "Though, I'm unsure how much more we can offer beyond finding her while hunting."

"That's okay," Michael said. "Sometimes even the smallest detail can be something we missed and could make a difference."

Johnny nodded in agreement as he and Chris began recounting the details to Deputy Thomas. They went through everything they knew, eager to get it all out and leave this unsettling place behind. The day had already delivered more than its fair share of horrors—images they knew would stick with them for a lifetime. Each word they shared felt like a step closer to getting away from the scene, from the body, and the eerie stillness of the swamp.

Meanwhile, Michael and Mark cautiously approached the spot where the woman's body lay intermingled with the cypress knees. The oppressive air thickened around them as they drew closer, and the reality of what they were about to witness weighed heavily. They had seen their share of challenging situations in law enforcement, but nothing could fully prepare them for this.

As they stepped into the clearing, the fog seemed to hang lower, almost as if it were trying to shroud the scene. The body was partially submerged in the murky water and tangled among the gnarled roots of the cypress trees. Her limbs were twisted unnaturally, and her bloated skin was barely visible beneath the grime and muck. The sight was worse than either of them had expected, the brutality of it stark and undeniable. It was the kind of scene that left a mark, the kind you carried with you long after you left.

Michael exhaled slowly, his jaw tightening as he tried to take it all in. Standing beside him, Mark remained silent, momentarily stunned by the grotesque reality of what they had walked into. They had heard Johnny and Chris describe the scene, but seeing it in person was entirely different. The raw, brutal nature of the situation made it clear that this wasn't just some tragic accident—something far more sinister had happened here.

Despite how they felt then, Michael and Mark knew they had a job to do. Michael instructed Mark to tape off the area while he radioed back to the station. They were going to need more assistance in this situation.

Fortunately, help was already on the way. Incidents like this were rare in a small town, and word didn't stay quiet for long. When something this serious happened, everyone with any connection to law enforcement or just a desire to see what was going on gathered to either lend a hand or satisfy their curiosity.

Michael knew it was only a matter of time before more people arrived, so he wasted no time photographing the scene while it was still undisturbed. He didn't think the body had been placed there from the land, but he wasn't taking any chances. To be thorough, he asked Thomas to record Johnny's and Chris's boot impressions to rule them out.

His initial thought was that someone had likely dumped the body into the bayou, and it had floated to this spot. As the water receded, the body became trapped in the cypress knees. However, Michael knew he needed more evidence before drawing any conclusions.

The medical examiners and coroner arrived at the scene, their expressions shifting to grim focus as they prepared for the task ahead. As they approached the body, the air grew thick with the unmistakable, nauseating stench of decay. The foul odor hit them like a wall, so overwhelming that a few of them instinctively gagged, hands moving to cover their noses and mouths. It was a smell they had encountered before, but it never became more manageable. The combination of the swamp's humidity and the state of the body made the air nearly unbearable.

Despite the urge to retreat, they pushed forward, knowing they had a job. With the stench hanging heavy around them, they worked quickly and efficiently. One examiner stood beside the body, pulling out a thermometer to take the temperature, while another snapped photos from every angle, ensuring that everything would be noticed in their documentation. The soft click of the camera was a stark contrast to the eerie quiet of the swamp.

As they worked, the examiners logged all the essential details into their notebooks, each movement precise and methodical. They knew they only had a limited window to gather the information they needed before moving the body to the morgue for a more thorough examination. The heat of the bayou and the rapid decomposition made this moment critical for preserving as much evidence as possible.

Standing a few feet away, the coroner flipped through paperwork, his face severe as he carefully logged the preliminary findings. Despite the unpleasantness of the scene, the group worked with practiced efficiency. Every piece of data—temperature readings, visual details, and the positioning of the body—was meticulously recorded for later analysis.

After completing the initial examination, the team faced the challenge of moving the body deeply entangled among the cypress stumps in the murky water. With their gnarled roots and protruding knees, the stumps had formed what looked like a natural tomb, trapping the woman's body in their twisted embrace. The process would require precision and care—any misstep could compromise the fragile evidence or damage the decaying remains.

Two examiners positioned themselves near the woman's upper body, each gently taking hold of an arm while the other two carefully grasped her legs. The body, bloated from its time in the water, was heavy and uncooperative, the limbs stiff from rigor mortis. With a slow, deliberate effort, they lifted her out of the swampy water, doing their best to avoid causing any more disruption to the scene.

The cypress roots made the task even more complicated, their knobby surfaces tugging at the body as if refusing to let go. But the team worked with steady hands; each movement deliberated as they navigated the challenging terrain. The saturated ground beneath them squished with every step, making it harder to find their footing, but they managed to shift the body away from the entangling roots and stumps that had trapped it for so long.

Once freed from the grip of the cypress stumps, they carefully carried the body across the uneven, swampy land to a flatter, drier area they had prepared for the body bag. The weight of the situation pressed down on them—not just the physical burden of moving the body but the emotional toll of handling such a grim task.

Now that the body had been carefully removed from the cypress stumps and murky water, the medical examiners had a clearer view and could begin taking additional photographs from various angles. She was completely nude and badly bruised. The scene was sad, and the gravity of the situation weighed heavily on them as they worked.

The woman's body lay on the dry patch of land, fully exposed to the examiners. Her blonde hair was matted and tangled, likely from being submerged in the bayou's muddy waters for an extended period. Her blue eyes, now dull and lifeless, seemed to stare vacantly at the overcast sky. She appeared to be about five feet tall, possibly a bit shorter or taller, though it was difficult to gauge with certainty in her current state. Her skin, pale and bloated from the water, was marred by dirt and debris from the swamp.

The left side of the woman's face was marred by significant bruising, the skin swollen and discolored, suggesting a forceful blow or some trauma. Her lower jaw was visibly misaligned and shifted unnaturally to the right, hinting at either a dislocation or a break. The deformity was subtle but clear, a detail that stood out amid the other injuries. It was impossible to say with certainty what had caused it, but the injury spoke of violence, and the full extent of the damage would only be revealed during the autopsy.

As the examiners continued their assessment, they noticed something even more telling—distinct marks encircling the woman's wrists. These were unmistakable signs of restraint. The rawness of the skin and the deep impressions indicated that she had been tied up, likely with some rope or cord. The fresh markings told one part of the story, but more chilling was revealed as they examined closer. Beneath the newer injuries, faint scarring wrapped around her wrists, evidence of older, healed wounds.

The presence of these older scars hinted at a grim possibility. This woman had likely been restrained not just in the final moments leading to her death but for an extended period beforehand. The scarring suggested she had been tied up repeatedly or over a long duration, with the ropes digging into her skin over time, leaving behind permanent damage. It painted a haunting picture of prolonged suffering, abuse, or captivity.

Her ankles bore the same troubling signs as her wrists—deep, circular impressions indicating she had been bound tightly. The marks wrapped entirely around each ankle, suggesting that they had been tied separately rather than together, as though she had been restrained in a position that prevented her from moving freely. The skin around the marks was raw, and in some places, the flesh seemed bruised, hinting that the restraints had likely been in place for a significant amount of time, cutting into her skin with enough pressure to leave lasting damage.

As the examiners moved on, they noted the extensive injuries across her back, buttocks, and the backs of her legs. The lacerations and abrasions varied in size and severity. Some cuts were shallow, likely caused by sharp branches or rough surfaces, while others appeared more deliberate, profound, and organized. These marks painted a disturbing picture of what could have happened to her. The injuries could have been caused by torture—perhaps inflicted by whoever had restrained her—or they might have been the result of her body being dragged or exposed to the rough, unforgiving terrain of the swamp.

The examiners couldn't yet determine if these wounds were caused by abuse or if they had occurred post-mortem as her body lay exposed to the elements. The swamp was full of hazards—sharp rocks, branches, and even wildlife—that could have contributed to the marks, but the possibility of torture couldn't be ruled out. The scene was too raw, the evidence too fresh, for them to draw any concrete conclusions.

Nonetheless, the medical team worked methodically, carefully photographing and recording each detail. They knew that every bruise, every cut, and every scar might hold clues to her story, and they didn't want to overlook anything. The answers they sought would come later, in the sterile environment of the morgue, where they could conduct a more thorough examination.

Once the examination was finished, the medical examiners carefully zipped up the body bag, sealing Jane Doe inside with a quiet, sad focus. The soft sound of the zipper felt heavy in the stillness of the bayou, signaling the end of this first step in uncovering the truth behind her death. Now, it was time to transport her to the morgue for a more thorough examination, where more details about her tragic fate might come to light.

The swampy terrain posed a challenge—there was no direct path to drive down to the bayou and no easy way to reach the scene by vehicle. The only option was to carry the body out by hand. The examiners prepared the stretcher, knowing they'd have to navigate the narrow, uneven levee alongside the canal. The levee was rough, the ground still damp and slick from the morning fog, making the trek back to the vehicles even more precarious.

Each examiner took their position around the stretcher, grabbing a corner. The weight of the body, combined with the rugged terrain, made the task physically demanding. Still, they lifted her carefully, mindful of preserving the evidence and maintaining dignity for the deceased. Slowly, they began the arduous journey back toward the waiting vehicles, their footsteps heavy but steady as they moved single file along the levee.

For everyone involved, this once-familiar part of the bayou would be forever tainted, the peaceful memories of countless hunts now overshadowed by the day's grim discovery. For years, this stretch of land had been a sanctuary—a place where the routine of hunting brought a sense of calm and tradition. But after today, the haunting image of the woman's body tangled among the cypress stumps would leave a deep scar in their minds, turning a once-comforting place into a scene of tragedy.

The weight of this day would follow them, coloring their memories of the bayou in a way that couldn't easily be shaken. It wouldn't just be the hunters who felt this—the examiners, the deputies, and anyone else who had been part of this discovery. For all of them, the bayou had transformed from a familiar hunting ground into a haunting reminder of the fragile line between life and death.

It would be a long time, if ever, before any of them would feel comfortable returning to this area. The joy and excitement they once felt when walking these trails would be replaced by a heaviness, knowing that the shadow of what they had witnessed would always linger. No matter how many seasons passed or hunts they experienced elsewhere, the sight of the woman lying among the cypress stumps, submerged in the swamp, would be forever imprinted in their minds—a reminder that even in the most familiar places, darkness can surface.

## Chapter 5

Leah lay motionless, her heart pounding as she heard a faint noise from across the room. The sound was unmistakable—the slow, deliberate turn of a doorknob, followed by the heavy, resounding click of the latch disengaging. A moment later, the grating screech of rusty hinges pierced the stillness, signaling a door opening in the darkness beyond her blindfold.

Panic surged through her. Unable to see anything through the thick fabric covering her eyes, she strained to listen for any other sounds, desperate to understand what was happening. But there was nothing, just the quiet hum of tension filling the room. The gag pressed against her lips, silencing her completely. Even if she wanted to scream or call out for help, she couldn't. All she could do was lie there, bound, vulnerable, and waiting.

In the silence that followed, Leah's mind raced. She could not know who had just entered the room or what they wanted. Fear clawed at her insides as she imagined the worst. The only thing she could think to do was remain still—perhaps if she didn't move, whoever had opened the door would leave her alone. Maybe they were checking on her, she told herself, trying to calm her rapid breathing. Perhaps they would take a quick look and then close the door, leaving her in the solitude of the room once more.

Unfortunately, Leah's hopes were quickly dashed. Instead of hearing the door close and the person leave, she caught the faint sound of footsteps—slow and deliberate—heading in her direction. The faint shuffle grew louder with each step, the sound of shoes against the floor echoing in the silent room. With each approaching footfall, Leah's dread deepened, her body instinctively tightening as her heart raced faster.

Her breath hitched in her throat, and she began to tremble uncontrollably. The closer the footsteps came, the more the fear twisted inside her like a tightening noose. She could not defend herself, speak, see, or escape. Completely helpless, Leah's mind raced with terrifying possibilities. Who was this person? What did they want? And, most hauntingly, what were they about to do to her?

The footsteps filled the room, but to her, it felt like it filled her entire world. Her body shook uncontrollably, betraying her fear as she lay bound and blindfolded. Every second felt like a slow-motion nightmare, each footstep closer to her a ticking reminder that her fate was no longer in her control.

Then, the footsteps stopped. The sudden silence was deafening, making her hyperaware of her shallow breathing and the pounding of her heart. Leah could feel the presence of someone near her—so close, the air seemed to thicken with their proximity—but she had no way of knowing exactly how close they stood. The blindfold robbed her of any visual clues, and the oppressive quiet only amplified the fear building inside her. She lay there, bound, gagged, and utterly vulnerable, waiting for the unknown to unfold.

Her mind spiraled into panic, thoughts racing uncontrollably. Is this it? Is this how it ends? Her situation hit her like a wave, cold and suffocating. She had always imagined death might come in some tragic but natural way—maybe an accident, perhaps illness. But not like this. Not bound hand and foot, blindfolded and gagged, entirely at the mercy of someone whose intentions she couldn't even begin to guess.

This was not how she had envisioned her end. In all the ways she had ever feared death, this scenario had never crossed her mind. The thought of dying this way—alone, defenseless, and terrified—was unbearable. The stillness around her felt like a dark intro, a moment frozen in time just before the storm. Leah braced herself for whatever was coming next, her body trembling, every nerve screaming with the fear of the unknown.

Leah next felt the unmistakable touch of a hand sliding up the back of her dress. It was slow, deliberate, and horrifying. Her entire body tensed as the hand moved with unsettling confidence, fingers brushing against her skin as they reached for the waistband of her panties. A surge of panic coursed through her as the fabric was slowly pulled down, inch by inch. The intimacy of the violation sent her into a mental spiral, her mind screaming questions she couldn't voice. What is happening? Why are they doing this?

She was frozen in terror, her limbs rigid, her heart pounding so violently it echoed in her ears. The gag stifled any cry for help, reducing her fear to muffled, breathless gasps. The blindfold made the act feel even more sinister, heightening the feeling of powerlessness. She couldn't see who was touching her, couldn't beg them to stop, couldn't even understand their intent—only the sickening sensation of her vulnerability being exploited.

Why? The question screamed inside her head, growing louder with every second. She felt trapped in her own body, suffocating under the weight of helplessness. Leah didn't want this—couldn't bear this—but what could she do?

Please, no, she begged, praying for some miracle. Tears stung her eyes beneath the blindfold, her body trembling uncontrollably.

Suddenly, Leah felt herself being lifted off the bed. Strong arms wrapped around her, and despite the panic surging through her, she remained still, helpless to resist. The sensation of being carried across the room sent her heart racing even faster. Her mind whirled with questions—Where are they taking me? What will they do next?—but she had no answers, only the fear of the unknown as the room felt endless and unfamiliar.

When the person set her down on a chair, the cold surface against her skin startled her. Confusion clouded her thoughts as she tried to make sense of the situation. She was sitting, but why? What did they want from her? Was she just meant to sit there in silence, bound and blindfolded, while her captor stood nearby, watching her? The uncertainty gnawed at her, and without the ability to see, her senses heightened, making every sound feel sharper and every pause more ominous.

Then, she heard footsteps again. The person was approaching, the soft thud of their shoes coming closer. Leah tensed, bracing herself for what she feared would be another violation or worse—some assault. Her body stiffened, preparing for the worst as she sensed the figure looming near her. She bit down hard on the gag, her breath coming in shallow gasps. The terror of not knowing what was coming next only added to her helplessness.

But before the person touched her, a toilet flushing echoed in the small space. Relief washed over her as the realization hit—she wasn't about to be assaulted again. Instead, they wanted her to relieve herself. The chair she had been placed on wasn't just a regular seat but the toilet.

The situation's embarrassment was overwhelming, but at least now she understood. In the fog of her fear, she had braced for the worst, only to find herself in a humiliating position. Her body trembled, not from the immediate terror she had expected but from the stark reality of her helplessness.

Leah's thoughts quickly shifted from fear to disgust as she grappled with what was happening. What kind of sick person does this? She wondered, her mind racing. Were they going to stand there and watch her as she relieved herself? Was this part of their twisted game? Is this what they get off on?

The idea of someone standing mere feet away, watching her in such a vulnerable moment, made it almost impossible to relax. At first, she couldn't go, her body frozen by the overwhelming mixture of fear, disgust, and humiliation. How am I supposed to do this? she thought, trying to block out the fact that someone was standing there, watching, waiting. Every second that passed seemed to stretch into eternity, and the pressure inside her was a cruel reminder of how trapped she was.

Her mind began to race as she assumed she would be reprimanded for her actions if she didn't go. It wasn't that she didn't have to go; Leah was just not used to going in front of others. She knew she had to do something soon, or she would lose the opportunity to go. She had to think of a way to do what this person wanted.

Desperation forced her mind to find a way through the situation. She remembered being in a similar predicament, though far less terrifying. She had been at a crowded event, an impossibly long women's bathroom line. Desperate, she'd marched into the men's room and used a urinal, uncaring of the strange looks she'd received. If I could do it then, I can do it now, she thought, trying to convince herself that this was no different.

Leah closed her eyes beneath the blindfold and took a deep breath, mentally distancing herself from the horror of her current reality. She told herself this was just another awkward moment, trying to find strength in the memory. It wasn't easy, but she managed to calm herself enough to focus on what she needed to do. Slowly, her body responded, and she was finally able to go, though every second felt like a violation of her dignity.

The good news was that Leah finally managed to relieve herself. However, she found herself wondering if she would ever stop. She had far more in her bladder than she'd expected, and it seemed to go on for longer than she anticipated.

As the relief washed over her, she almost forgot, for a fleeting moment, that someone was standing there, watching her in this humiliating state. At this point, she didn't care anymore. The situation had drained her of any sense of control or dignity. She figured she likely wouldn't leave this alive, and this moment felt like the lowest point of what had already become a nightmare.

Now that she had finished, with only a few lingering drops remaining, Leah wondered what would come next. Would the person carry her back to the bed? Would they leave her alone? Why weren't they saying anything?

Before she could form another thought, a sudden, unwelcome sensation shot through her body—a hand sliding between her legs. Panic surged, her instincts taking over before her mind could catch up. Without thinking, Leah slammed her legs shut, trapping the hand between her thighs. The shock of the contact, the violation, left her reeling.

Leah felt the hand trying to pull away, struggling to free itself from where it was trapped between her tightly clamped legs. Her body had instinctively locked up, and despite knowing she should release the hand, her mind was in full-blown panic mode, unable to let go. Every muscle in her body was tense, her fear so overwhelming that she couldn't control her reactions. She knew of her dangerous situation, but her body wasn't listening. Her instincts had utterly taken over, overriding any rational thought.

I'm making this worse, she thought in terror, but even knowing that she couldn't bring herself to release the grip her legs had on the hand. The panic was too strong, her fear too paralyzing. Her mind was screaming at her to do something, but all she could do was hold on, helpless in the face of her terror.

Then, suddenly, she felt it. A sharp smack on the right side of her hip. It wasn't hard enough to hurt but was firm, an unmistakable warning. The message was clear—they were still in control. The smack reminded her that, despite her instinctive resistance, they had the upper hand. Yet, even with that reminder, Leah couldn't release the hand. Her body was locked in a state of sheer panic, unable to react as her mind knew she should.

Before she could fully process the situation, another smack landed in the same spot. This one carried more force, driving the point home that her captor wouldn't tolerate her resistance much longer. The sensation was jarring, and though it didn't cause pain, it sent a chilling message through her body.

The message was unmistakable: submit, or the punishment would escalate. Each smack had been a warning, and Leah could feel the unspoken threat in the air. She didn't want to anger her captor further or make an already horrifying situation even worse. Her instincts, fueled by fear, finally took over. With trembling hesitation, she unclenched her legs and released the hand. All she wanted was for this nightmare to end, for this moment to be over as quickly as possible.

Even though fear had driven her to release the hand trapped between her legs, another sensation began to creep in, one she wasn't prepared for—desire. Despite the terror and helplessness of the moment, something about the situation stirred a part of her that wanted the hand to stay there. The smacks on her right side, though meant to control and dominate, had just enough sting to send an unexpected thrill through her body. Each sharp tingle excited her in a way she didn't understand, even as she remained trapped under someone else's control.

The fear of the unknown, of being unable to see what was coming next, and the submission of being entirely at the mercy of another person sent shivers up and down her spine. It was a strange, confusing cocktail of emotions—one moment, she was terrified; the next, a dark curiosity gripped her, making her wonder what might happen next. Her body reacted in ways she didn't want it to, betraying the panic that gripped her mind. The lack of control, the complete surrender to whatever came next, stirred something profound inside her that she couldn't quite push away.

As the person's hand finally retracted, Leah felt it brush against her most intimate area. The contact, brief as it was, sent a wave of sensation through her, and despite the horror of her situation, her body responded in a way that made her feel ashamed. Heat pooled inside her, and the tension she had built up transformed into something she wasn't prepared to feel. Why am I feeling this? she wondered, her thoughts racing.

Here she was, tied up, blindfolded, and gagged, under someone else's control, and yet part of her was being stirred by it. It didn't make sense, and yet the sensations were undeniable. The confusion overwhelmed her—What's wrong with me?—but she couldn't deny how her body responded. Each brush of the hand, each smack on her hip, left her conflicted, torn between fear and the unsettling excitement of submission.

She felt lifted again before Leah could process whether she thought right or wrong. Her assailant whisked her away from the chair without a word, carrying her effortlessly across the room. Her body tensed, expecting the worst, but instead of rough treatment, she was laid gently back onto the bed. The softness of the mattress beneath her was a jarring contrast to the tension inside her. She lay still, her senses heightened, trying to anticipate what was coming next.

Her mind raced, consumed with questions. Would this person finally take advantage of her in this vulnerable state? The thought terrified her but also stirred something deep within, a tangled mess of emotions she wasn't sure how to sort out. An undeniable part of her wanted something to happen, an instinctual craving for release from the storm of fear and desire swirling inside her. Her body, still reacting to the mix of submission and uncertainty, left her feeling conflicted.

Her emotions were like a tightly wound knot—fear, desire, helplessness, and confusion all wrapped up together. She knew she couldn't stop whatever was coming. She was bound, blindfolded, and gagged, entirely at the mercy of her captor. The realization that she had no control should have only deepened her terror, but instead, it created a strange acceptance. This is happening. I can't stop it.

But what unsettled her most was the question that hovered at the edge of her thoughts: If I had the chance to stop this, would I? Part of her, the rational part, screamed yes—she would do anything to prevent this violation. Yet another part, the part that felt drawn to the powerlessness of her situation, wondered if she would genuinely resist if given the opportunity. The thought disturbed her, making her ashamed, yet she couldn't fully push it away.

Leah lay there, her body betraying her mind, her heart pounding in her chest. She waited, unsure of what was about to happen and how she would react when it did.

## Chapter 6

Beau Benoit stirred awake at around three in the morning, the quiet darkness of his home still wrapped in the early hours. It was a familiar routine that began his much-anticipated time off. He stretched briefly before heading into the kitchen, where he took a moment to brew himself a pot of Community Coffee. The aroma filled the small space, comforting in its routine, while he prepared a simple breakfast—eggs, toast, and sausage, enough to fuel the long day ahead.

Today, Beau planned to get out on the water before sunrise, eager to check the trotlines he'd set the night before. Fishing had always been his way of unwinding, and the thought of spending the early hours on the peaceful bayou, with nothing but the sound of the water and the hum of his boat, filled him with anticipation. His morning routine was simple: fish a little, pull in any catfish or bass that had taken his bait, then retrieve his lines and head back home to Lake Arthur, Louisiana.

Lake Arthur was a quiet, small town where life moved comfortably and unhurriedly. Nestled along the shores of the largest natural lake in southern Louisiana, the city took its name from the very body of water that defined its character. The lake was the heartbeat of the community, offering endless opportunities for fishing, shrimping, and boating. Lake Arthur was the perfect place to call home for those who enjoyed casting a line or working on shrimp boats.

But the town's connection to the lake was more than just practical. Every year, Lake Arthur hosted a renowned sailboat regatta, a much-anticipated event that drew visitors from miles around. The regatta transformed the typically calm lake into a vibrant scene with colorful sails and friendly competition. Boat owners and spectators gathered to enjoy the camaraderie, food, and, of course, the beauty of the lake. It was more than just a race—a celebration of Cajun traditions, a time for old friends to reconnect and for the community to revel in the simple joys of life on the water.

Lake Arthur was steeped in Cajun culture, and that richness could be felt in every aspect of life there. Whether it was the mouth-watering crawfish boils, gumbo, and jambalaya served at gatherings or the lively sounds of zydeco music floating through the air during festivals, the town proudly held onto its heritage. The people of Lake Arthur loved to share these traditions with anyone who passed through, always eager to showcase the warmth and vibrancy of their way of life.

While Lake Arthur was a charming place to visit, it was an even better place to fish. The calm, sprawling waters of the lake were home to bass, catfish, and a variety of other freshwater species, making it a haven for anglers. Whether you were an experienced fisherman or just looking to enjoy a quiet day by the water, Lake Arthur had everything you could ask for. The lake, framed by towering cypress trees and teeming with wildlife, provided the perfect backdrop for a day of peaceful fishing.

For Beau, these fishing trips weren't just a pastime—they were a vital escape from his demanding life as a Derrickhand on the oil rigs. His fourteen-day shifts were physically exhausting, filled with long hours of climbing, handling heavy equipment, and ensuring the rig ran smoothly. The job required skill and endurance, as he balanced on platforms, managed the drill pipe, and monitored the flow of drilling fluids. It was dangerous, dirty work, and after two weeks straight, Beau often felt utterly drained. Once his shift was up, he'd return home, barely able to muster the energy for anything other than sleeping off the fatigue. The first few days back on land were spent simply recuperating—catching up on rest, eating meals that weren't prepared in the rig's kitchen, and enjoying the peaceful quiet of his small town. But once he felt himself return to life, his mind turned to the bayou.

Beau looked like a man shaped by years of hard work under the unforgiving Louisiana sun. His build was average, but it was clear that his strength came from the physical demands of his job, his muscles hardened by the grueling work on the oil rigs. At first glance, you might peg him for his early fifties, though he was only in his early forties. The long hours on the rig, combined with the constant exposure to the elements, gave a roughness to his skin that made him appear older than his years. His sun-kissed complexion was a testament to a life lived outdoors, working with his hands and enduring the heat and humidity that were constant companions in this part of the world.

Beau stood about six feet tall, with salt-and-pepper hair that had once been dark brown, now streaked with the grays that time and toil had brought. His hair was cropped short, practical for his line of work, and always hidden under a worn baseball cap when he was on the water or working on the rig. His brown eyes carried a calmness, a sense of quiet strength, but they also hinted at the weariness from years of long shifts, early mornings, and hard days. A thick mustache sat above his weathered lips, a defining feature he'd had for as long as anyone could remember.

When you see Beau around town, you can always count on him to dress relatively simply. His wardrobe rarely changed—he was a man who preferred practicality over fashion. Most days, he wore a pair of overalls over a plain T-shirt, a style he stuck to for comfort and ease. Today was no different. The denim overalls were a staple in his wardrobe, sturdy enough for a long day on the water yet comfortable enough to wear from dawn to dusk. He liked its simplicity, never caring much about anything fancy or trendy. Beau had little time or patience for frills or complications in life, and his clothing reflected that.

Of course, today was the same for Beau. After finishing breakfast, he slipped into his usual outfit—a pair of comfortable overalls and a simple T-shirt—and stepped outside into the predawn darkness, ready for his fishing trip. The air was still cool, with only the faintest hint of light on the horizon. Though it was dark, Beau knew the way to his truck by heart. The boat was already hooked up to the trailer and ready to head to the dock on Third Street.

The short drive through Lake Arthur's quiet, sleeping town was peaceful. As he passed through the dimly lit streets, the town was still in its slumber, with only the occasional street lamp casting a soft glow. Beau liked these early morning hours when the world was quiet and the day hadn't yet begun for most. The water, he knew, would be just as peaceful.

When he arrived at the boat dock, he skillfully backed the trailer down the ramp and into the water—years of practice had made this routine second nature for him. The aluminum boat, about twelve feet long, was simple and had no frills—just like Beau liked it. With an essential motor on the back, it wasn't anything fancy, but it got the job done. For Beau, fishing wasn't about flash or luxury; it was about getting out on the water and losing himself in the quiet rhythm of the bayou.

After securely tying the boat to the dock, Beau parked his truck and trailer in the parking lot. The lot was empty, with just a few shadows cast by the early morning moonlight. He grabbed the essentials from the back of his truck: an ice chest for the day's catch and a spare gas can in case he needed it later.

Once Beau was settled in the boat, he untied it from the dock and set off toward his favorite fishing spot. His boat wasn't flashy—no sleek fiberglass or glittery paint jobs with steering wheels and consoles. It was just a plain aluminum rig, practical and unassuming, with simple bench seats and a small motor that he steered from the back. It wasn't built for speed or style, but it was perfect for navigating the winding bayous and rivers of the area. That's all Beau needed—a reliable boat to get him where the fish were biting.

Beau had to navigate through familiar waterways to reach his usual fishing spot. He guided the boat down a narrow causeway, the stillness of the early morning broken only by the quiet hum of the motor and the gentle ripple of the water under the hull. The air was crisp and cool, and the mist hung low over the water, giving the landscape a dreamlike quality. The path took him around Gaithes Point, a place he'd passed hundreds of times over the years, its marshy edges lined with tall grasses swaying in the soft breeze.

From there, he continued eastward, passing Laurents Point as the boat glided effortlessly through the calm water. The sky was starting to brighten now, the first hints of dawn creeping over the horizon, casting a faint glow on the lake's surface. As Beau moved closer to the bridge where the Mermentau River spilled into Lake Arthur, the current picked up slightly, indicating that he was nearing his desolation.

He maneuvered through the winding turns of the Mermentau River, a route he could have navigated blindfolded after so many years of fishing these waters. The river snaked its way through the landscape, the banks lined with cypress trees whose roots dipped into the water, creating a natural maze of vegetation. The thick roots jutted out, occasionally narrowing the passage, but Beau knew how to guide his boat through the turns without a hitch.

After a peaceful journey, Beau finally reached the junction where Bayou Queue De Tortue met the Mermentau River. It was the perfect spot—secluded and tucked away from any boat traffic, just wide enough for him to navigate through comfortably. Here, he could fish in solitude, away from the noise and distractions of the world.

The bayou's winding path didn't bother him at all. He wasn't in a rush; he had the entire day ahead of him. His only priority was reaching the trotlines he'd set to see if they had caught anything. Out here, time moved slowly, and that's precisely how Beau liked it.

After traveling for about fifteen or twenty minutes, Beau finally arrived at the spot where he'd placed his trotlines the day before. The location was ideal, tucked away in a quiet bayou bend where he'd fished many times. His trotlines weren't anything fancy—just a simple string about ten feet long, with eight smaller lines hanging down, each with a hook. He'd baited them the night before, hoping the fish would have taken the bait overnight.

As Beau began pulling up the first trotline, he could feel the weight, a sure sign that something had been caught. Excitement buzzed through him—this was the part he looked forward to most, that moment of discovery. With a firm tug, he brought the line-up, revealing his first catch of the day: a nice, hefty catfish on the first hook. A grin spread across his face; he could imagine frying it up later.

The following two hooks were empty, but he felt the familiar tug of more fish on the line. The remaining hooks yielded two more good-sized catfish, their sleek, whiskered bodies wriggling as they came into view. Three fish in total—not bad for the first line he checked.

It was already shaping up to be a good day. With three fish in the ice chest, Beau was off to a great start, and the morning had barely begun. He wasted no time securing the fish in the cooler, then quickly rebaited the empty hooks, preparing the trotline for another round while he checked the other lines.

Beau checked the next two trotlines, and the haul did not disappoint. He pulled another five good-sized fish between the two lines, adding to his already solid start to his day. After quickly rebaiting the hooks, he ventured further up the bayou for some bass fishing. He figured he'd spend an hour or two casting his line before circling back to recheck the trotlines on his way home.

Navigating the twisting, narrow turns of the bayou for another fifteen minutes, Beau felt at ease. The morning was still cool, the air crisp and fresh, and the mist hanging over the water had started to lift. As he reached a familiar fishing spot tucked away from the main channels, he cut the motor and let the boat drift quietly. The water was calm, barely a ripple on the surface, and the world around him was still.

One of his favorite spots was a quiet little pocket of the bayou where the trees formed a natural canopy overhead, their branches dipping low into the water. The only sounds were the distant chirping of birds and the occasional rustle of wind through the cypress trees. Beau grabbed his rod and reel, casting his line out into the water with practiced ease. He wasn't a trophy-winning bass fisherman by any means, but he loved the sport for the challenge it presented.

Standing in the boat, Beau began his familiar routine. He cast the line out, gave it a little jig as he reeled it in, watched the lure dance through the water, and cast again. Something was calming about the repetitive motion: the line flew through the air and landed with a soft plop on the water's surface. Each cast held the promise of a catch, but for Beau, it was about more than the fish. The solitude, connection to nature, and peace came from being out on the water with nothing but the sounds of the bayou surrounding him.

As Beau continued fishing, enjoying the peace of the morning, he made the kind of mistake every fisherman makes from time to time: casting too close to the cypress stumps. His line snagged, and as he tried to reel it in, he realized the lure was stuck. Frustration bubbled up. He wasn't about to lose one of his favorite lures—especially not one he'd spent eight dollars on. The bayou gods weren't getting a donation from him today.

The untethered and unanchored boat made it easier to deal with the situation. Beau began reeling in the line, slowly pulling his boat toward the cluster of stumps where the lure had lodged. His plan was simple: get as close to the stump as possible, reach into the water, and dislodge the lure. He'd done it before and wasn't too concerned about it.

When Beau finally reached the set of stumps, he leaned over the side of the boat, following the line with his hand into the murky water, hoping the lure wasn't too deep. As his fingers traced down the fishing line, he realized the lure was more profound than anticipated. He laid down in the boat to get better reach, letting part of his upper body hang over the edge. The water lapped quietly against the hull as he stretched his arm down, determined to retrieve his lost lure.

Finally, his fingers grazed the lure. He tugged on it gently, trying to free it from the roots. But just as he gave it a stronger pull, something unexpected happened that made his heart leap into his throat. A ghostly pale figure emerged from beneath the surface of the water. It wasn't just debris or a hollow log, as he had first thought. It was a woman's body, floating lifelessly, suddenly rising between the cypress stumps.

The shock hit Beau like a bolt of lightning. His breath caught, and fear shot through him. He scrambled backward, his body reacting instinctively, trying to distance himself from the horrifying sight. His heart pounded in his chest, adrenaline rushing through his veins as he fought to get away from the floating corpse. The sight of her, pale and bloated from the water, bobbing between the stumps, was like something out of a nightmare—a nightmare he was now living.

Beau's hands shook, and his mind raced. The woman's body was tangled in the roots, her limbs stiff and unnatural. He had never imagined his quiet day of fishing would turn into something so horrific. He couldn't move fast enough, his body scrambling in the boat to get away from the water, from the image that would now be seared into his mind. He had seen death before, but this—this was something else. The image of the body floating eerily in the swamp was something he knew he would never forget. The horror of the moment would haunt him for many nights to come, invading his dreams and turning his once peaceful bayou into a place of nightmares.

## Chapter 7

Beau's mind was spinning, his heart racing uncontrollably as he sat frozen in the boat. The sight of the woman's lifeless body, pale and bloated, floating among the cypress stumps paralyzed him with fear. He knew he had to do anything, but his body refused to cooperate. It was as if the shock of finding the body had short-circuited his ability to think clearly. His hands trembled as he gripped the side of the boat, staring at the woman's still form, unable to tear his eyes away.

His mind screamed at him to move, to get help, but his body remained locked in place. He couldn't look away from her, the water gently rocking her lifeless body, her pale skin in stark contrast to the dark, murky bayou. It was unreal, like something out of a nightmare, yet it was happening before him. His thoughts raced, trying to make sense of the horror he had stumbled upon. How did she end up here? What happened to her? Questions tumbled through his mind, but no answers came.

Beau had spent his life fishing these waters, navigating the twists and turns of the bayou, and never once had he encountered anything like this. This wasn't supposed to happen here, in this peaceful, remote part of Louisiana. The swamp was a quiet place where life slowed down. But now, it had become something darker, something sinister.

His heart pounded in his chest as the initial shock slowly gave way to a creeping sense of dread. He knew he couldn't leave her there, floating between the cypress stumps like a ghostly figure. Yet, he couldn't move. His muscles felt tight, locked by fear, as if the weight of the situation had rooted him in place. The silence of the bayou, once comforting, now seemed oppressive, amplifying his isolation. No one was around for miles, just him, the boat, and the body.

The fear that gripped him wasn't just from the sight of the dead woman—it was the realization that he was utterly alone out here, with no immediate help. The weight of responsibility pressed down on him, yet he couldn't force himself to act. His mind was a blur of panicked thoughts, running in circles as he tried to comprehend what had happened to her. Was it an accident? Had someone done this to her? What if someone did this to her, and they were still out here?

With that final terrifying thought—that someone could be watching him—Beau snapped out of his frozen state. Panic flooded his system, pushing him into action. Without hesitation, he reached for the boat's motor, his fingers trembling as he cranked it to life. The engine roared, and he didn't waste another second. He tore through the water, speeding away from the scene as fast as the boat could carry him.

The usually calm and winding bayou, with its familiar twists and turns, became a blur as he navigated it at a speed he had never attempted. Beau's heart pounded as he gripped the steering handle tightly, his eyes darting between the water ahead and the shadowy edges of the bayou. Every gnarled tree root and hidden corner now seemed menacing, as if the quiet swamp was hiding something—or someone—in its depths. The thought of someone lurking, watching him as he found the body, sent shivers down his spine, fueling his urgency.

His mind raced as fast as the boat, playing out every worst-case scenario. What if there was someone out there? What if they knew I saw her? The fear gnawed at him, driving him to push the boat even harder through the narrow channels. The once serene bayou had transformed into a place of terror, and Beau did not intend to discover what more it could reveal.

With no form of communication that could reach help from this remote area, Beau knew he had no choice but to make it back to Lake Arthur as quickly as possible. The isolation that had once been comforting now felt like a dangerous trap. His only option was to get back to town and alert the authorities.

The journey back felt like an eternity, even as the boat sped through the winding waterways. His mind kept flashing back to the woman's lifeless body, floating between the cypress stumps, her image burned into his memory. But he couldn't think about that now—he had to focus on getting help, getting out of the bayou and into safety.

Finally, as the familiar waterfront of Lake Arthur came into view, Beau let out a breath he hadn't realized he'd been holding. Relief mixed with lingering fear as he slowed the boat down, pulling it toward the dock with shaky hands. He glanced around, scanning the area, still half-expecting someone to be following him, though the waters behind him were empty.

Fortunately, the Lake Arthur Police Department was close to the waterfront, only a short distance from where he would dock. Beau secured the boat and jumped out, his legs still trembling from the shock. He quickly ran towards the police department to get help.

Beau burst through the doors of the Lake Arthur Police Department, nearly colliding with Officer Blayne Guidry in his desperate rush to get help. The impact startled Blayne, who barely sidestepped to avoid being knocked over.

"Whoa, Beau! What's going on?" Blayne asked, his voice filled with concern as he steadied himself.

Blayne and Beau knew each other well, having grown up in Lake Arthur. They'd attended the same schools, played football side by side, and shared years of memories in their tight-knit community. Seeing Beau so frantic immediately sent alarm bells ringing in Blayne's head.

"Blayne, you gotta come—I need help!" Beau shouted, his voice frantic, his breaths coming in short, uneven gasps as if the weight of what he had just experienced was squeezing the air out of his lungs.

"Hold on, slow down," Blayne said, placing a hand on Beau's shoulder to calm him. "What's the rush, man? You look like you've seen a ghost or something."

Beau's eyes widened, his face pale and drenched in sweat. "Blayne, I —I saw a dead body," he blurted out, his voice cracking with panic.

Blayne froze for a moment, the words hanging in the air between them. "What? A dead body?" he repeated, trying to process the shock of what Beau had just said.

Beau nodded frantically, his hands shaking. "Out in the bayou, between the cypress stumps—I was fishing and saw her! Just floating there, dead! You have to come now!" His voice was a mixture of terror and urgency, every word pushing Blayne closer to action.

"Alright, alright, calm down," Blayne said, trying to keep his mind focused as the gravity of the situation set in. He glanced at the dispatcher behind him before returning to Beau, his pulse quickening. "Where did you find the body?"

"In Bayou Queue De Tortue. I was pulling up a snagged lure when she popped up—Blayne, we need to go now!" Beau's words came in a rush, the moment's horror still etched into his face.

"Okay, we'll get a team together and head out there right away," Blayne said, quickly switching into work mode. He motioned to the others in the department. "Tell the chief—we've got an emergency in the bayou.

Like Beau, Blayne knew the Bayou Queue De Tortue area like the back of his hand. He had spent countless hours on those waters, casting lines and navigating the winding turns of the bayou since childhood. His father had first introduced him to fishing there, and as soon as Blayne was old enough to handle a boat by himself, he ventured out regularly, drawn to the quiet beauty and solitude of the place. The bayou held fond memories for him—weekends spent with family, quiet moments with nothing but the sound of the water and the breeze through the cypress trees.

But never, in all those years, had Blayne ever imagined something like this happening. The thought of a dead body being found in the peaceful waters he had grown up exploring seemed surreal, like something from a nightmare. Despite the shock Beau had brought with him, Blayne knew they had to act quickly. The clock was ticking, and any delay could mean the loss of crucial evidence.

His instincts as an officer kicked in. "We need to call the Vermilion Parish Sheriff's Department before we head out," Blayne said, calm but firm. "That bayou falls under their jurisdiction."

The dispatcher, already keyed into the situation's urgency, gave Blayne a quick nod and picked up the phone to notify the sheriff's department. Blayne knew the importance of bringing in the proper authorities, especially with something this serious. Vermilion Parish had the resources to investigate properly, and Blayne didn't want to overstep, but he also knew time was of the essence.

"Let them know we're heading out now, but we won't touch anything," Blayne added, leaning into the dispatcher's desk. "We'll meet them at the scene."

As the dispatcher made the call, Blayne turned back to Beau, whose face was still pale and anxious. "They'll meet us out there," Blayne reassured him. "We'll guide them to the spot, but we've got to be careful not to disturb anything. They'll handle the investigation."

Blayne understood how delicate these situations were. Evidence in the bayou could disappear quickly—washed away by the water, disturbed by wildlife, or lost to the environment and every second counted. He grabbed his gear, motioning to Beau to follow. There was no time to waste.

They hurried out of the police department, and Blayne quickly jumped into Beau's boat. Beau, still shaken but focused, fired up the engine and steered the boat back toward the spot where he had discovered the body. Several other officers followed behind them in two boats, each understanding the situation's urgency. The ordinarily peaceful waters of the bayou now held a somber weight as they raced to the scene.

To an outsider, the swamps along the bayou all looked eerily similar—an endless maze of cypress trees, hanging moss, and winding water channels. No clear-cut landmarks, street signs, or definitive markers indicated where you were. It wasn't the kind of place you could describe in straightforward terms. You couldn't just say, "Turn left at the big oak tree," because dozens of big trees looked the same to an untrained eye. The bayou's twisting paths were a mystery to most.

But to people like Beau and Blayne—Cajuns born and raised in these swamps—the waters held their logic. There were landmarks if you knew how to see them. The way the roots of a particular tree dipped into the water or how a specific bend in the bayou curved a little sharper than others. The shape of a specific tree, maybe the way its branches reached out or how the moss hung in thicker drapes. These subtle differences told them exactly where they were. They navigated by instinct, guided by memories of past trips and the quiet familiarity of the bayou.

Beau and Blayne shared that same sense of place, a knowledge passed down through generations of people who had lived and worked these waters. They could tell where they were by the slight changes in the landscape, things an ordinary person might never notice. The cypress trees seemed to whisper directions, their twisted roots and knotted trunks acting as signposts in the watery wilderness.

As they neared the area, Beau throttled back the engine, the boat's pace slowing to a quiet hum as it glided through the water. He wanted to reduce the wake, keeping the scene undisturbed. Once comforting, the oppressive silence of the bayou now felt ominous, the stillness magnifying the gravity of what lay ahead. Beau's pulse quickened as they approached the spot where he had seen the body. He knew exactly where it was, but seeing it again made his stomach churn.

"Blayne, the body is right over there," Beau said, his voice low but filled with tension. His eyes were locked on a small patch of water near the bank.

Blayne scanned the area, but the murky water and dense growth of cypress trees made it hard to distinguish anything. "Where?" he asked, turning in Beau's direction. His eyes narrowed as he tried to focus.

"Right over there next to the bank, between the cypress knees," Beau repeated, his voice tight, pointing toward the tangled mass of roots jutting out of the water.

Blayne quickly swiveled his head, following Beau's outstretched arm, and then he saw it—just as Beau had described. Floating eerily still between the gnarled cypress knees was a woman's body. Her pale skin was ghostly against the dark water, and her limbs drifted slightly, caught between the roots that seemed to cradle her like some grotesque offering to the swamp.

A cold knot formed in Blayne's stomach as the reality of the situation hit him. Seeing the body, lifeless and tangled in the swamp's natural roots, sent a chill down his spine. The bayou, once a place of serenity for both men, now felt like a sinister force holding this dark secret in its grasp.

The woman's body appeared bloated, her face pale and unrecognizable from the effects of the water. Her body was naked, and her hair floated like dark ribbons around her head. The cypress knees seemed to have trapped her there, her body gently bobbing with the slight movement of the water, yet tethered by the twisted roots. The sight was haunting, and the stillness around her only amplified the horror.

For a moment, Blayne couldn't speak. His eyes lingered on the body, the details of the scene embedding themselves in his mind. This wasn't just another call—this was something that would stay with him for a long time. He knew they had to be careful not to disturb the area, but seeing the woman like this, so helplessly entangled in the swamp, made him feel an urgent need to act.

"Jesus," Blayne finally muttered under his breath. He quickly reached for his radio, signaling the officers in the other boats. "We've found the body," he said into the receiver, his voice steady but low. "Looks like she's caught up in the cypress knees—just as Beau said."

Next, he called back to the police station, his voice measured but urgent. Blayne needed to give a better description of their location than the vague directions Beau had provided earlier. The bayou was a labyrinth of waterways, and he wanted to ensure the sheriff's department could pinpoint precisely where they were to meet them at the scene.

"Dispatch, this is Officer Guidry," Blayne spoke into the radio, his eyes fixed on the body floating in the cypress knees as he gave more precise instructions. "We're about four miles into Bayou Queue De Tortue from where it meets the Mermentau River. Let the sheriff's department know we're between two large clusters of cypress stumps. Tell them to follow the sound of our engines if needed; we'll guide them in."

As soon as the message was relayed, Blayne turned to the other officers who had arrived in the boats behind them. They hadn't yet approached the scene, keeping a respectful distance, but were waiting for instructions. Blayne knew the importance of securing the area for preserving evidence and because word would spread fast in a small town like Lake Arthur. The moment people with police scanners picked up on the discovery of a body, curious onlookers would swarm the area, eager to catch a glimpse of the dreadful scene.

"We need to rope off the area around the body," Blayne called out to the officers in the other boats. His tone was authoritative but calm, a steady hand guiding them through the grim task. "We don't need a huge perimeter, just enough to preserve the scene. Be careful around the cypress roots—don't disturb anything."

The officers nodded and immediately went to work. They carefully anchored ropes between the boats and trees, sectioning off the area around the body. The swampy terrain made it challenging, but they knew it had to be done; every minute that passed increased the risk of contamination—whether by the water, wildlife, or, worse, the swarm of people who would inevitably come to gawk.

Blayne's mind raced, thinking ahead to what would happen next. They were in the heart of Cajun country, where news traveled faster than anywhere else. It wouldn't be long before the entire town knew about the discovery, and in a place where very little happened on a day-to-day basis, this would draw people in like moths to a flame. He could already imagine the scene—a crowd of curious onlookers, some with cameras, others just wanting to catch a glimpse of the woman who had met her tragic fate.

"Let's make sure no one gets too close," Blayne said, giving a final instruction to his team. "We don't want to lose evidence or disturb anything before the sheriff's department arrives. We'll need to secure the scene until they arrive."

The officers, understanding the gravity of the situation, worked efficiently to create a clear boundary around the body. Blayne took a deep breath, glancing at Beau, who still sat in the boat nearby, his face pale and eyes wide, clearly shaken by the morning events.

"You did the right thing," Blayne said quietly, walking over to Beau. "We'll handle this now."

Beau nodded, but Blayne could see the haunted look in his eyes. No amount of reassurance would erase the image of the body from his mind, nor the nightmare that would undoubtedly follow him long after this day was over. The bayou, once a sanctuary for both of them, had taken on a new, sinister presence—a place where dark secrets were uncovered and life and death intertwined in ways neither man had expected.

## Chapter 8

The news didn't take long to spread like wildfire around Lake Arthur and the surrounding small towns. The discovery of a body in the bayou sent shock waves through the community, igniting a sense of responsibility. Before anyone could fully grasp what had happened, boats began showing up—people eager to assist in any way they could. This incident captured not just everyone's attention but also their sense of duty. The locals were determined to play their part in the unfolding drama in their backyard.

Boats of all sizes started to appear, their owners craning their necks, trying to glimpse the scene between the cypress trees. Once still and quiet, the bayou was buzzing with the hum of outboard motors and whispers of speculation. Everyone, united in their determination to uncover the truth about the poor woman Beau had discovered, was converging on the swamp, resolved to find answers. This unity in the face of a shocking discovery was a testament to the strength of our community.

Fortunately, the police had anticipated this and were quick to act. Officers had already moved out in both directions along the bayou, setting up barricades to block off the crime scene from the gathering crowd. Only those directly involved in the investigation were allowed to do so. It wasn't easy, but they were unwavering in protecting the scene from contamination and preserving any evidence that could lead to answers. Their steadfast commitment to their duty was reassuring amid the chaos.

"Turn it around, folks, this is a restricted area," an officer shouted, waving off a boat full of locals who had motored up too close, trying to get a better look.

The officers were stretched thin, doing their best to keep the curious townsfolk at bay. Some people were persistent, arguing that they just wanted to see what was happening, but the police held firm. No one was getting through unless they had a reason to be there. Still, the scene turned into a spectacle, with more boats arriving by the minute, and the quiet bayou transformed into a hub of activity.

The police from Lake Arthur finally had some assistance controlling the crowd once the local Game Wardens arrived. They had been out patrolling the bayou that morning and, like everyone else, had heard the commotion across the radios. If they were being honest, their initial interest was more out of curiosity than duty—they wanted to see what the buzz was about. But their professional instincts kicked in once they arrived, and they immediately offered to help. Their swift and professional response was a testament to their dedication to their duty and earned them the respect of all present.

The game wardens worked with the police, helping to barricade the bayou from the onlookers. They positioned their boats strategically, blocking key access points along the waterway, and ensured that no one got too close to the body or the investigators. While their presence lent an additional layer of authority, it also showed that even those accustomed to the bayou's routine dangers were drawn in by the extraordinary nature of this discovery.

Like everyone else, the bayou was usually a place of peace for the game wardens. There, they dealt with illegal hunting or fishing, the occasional missing person, or accidents. Finding a body in such a grim, unnatural state was unsettling, even to them. The situation was becoming more surreal by the minute, and the growing crowd of boats added to the tense atmosphere.

As they helped secure the scene, they couldn't help but exchange whispers among themselves. Like everyone else, they were curious. Who was she? How had this happened? The answers were still far off, but they focused on securing the area. The bayou, for the moment, was more than just a stretch of water—it was now the center of a grim investigation, with everyone watching and waiting for the truth to be uncovered.

After about an hour of waiting, the Vermilion Parish Sheriff's

Department finally arrived. They had a much longer trek down the winding bayou to reach the spot where the body had been discovered compared to the local Lake Arthur police, who had responded quickly from closer by. As their boats approached, there was no mistaking them. Their vessels were marked, with the sheriff's department logos emblazoned on the sides, and their lights flashed brightly, cutting through the growing crowd of curious onlookers.

"Well, I take it we've made it to the right spot," one of the sheriff's deputies remarked as they pulled up in their boats.

"What gave it away?" one of the Lake Arthur officers joked, gesturing to the vast number of boats clustered in the area.

"The fact that I've never seen this many boats in one spot back here in my life," the deputy replied, shaking his head. "Took us a minute to even get through them all, and that's with the lights flashing."

"Yeah, as soon as the word went out across the radios, it spread like wildfire," the Lake Arthur officer responded. "Half the town's probably out here by now."

"I hear you," the deputy said, glancing over the crowd of boats, a mix of frustration and understanding in his tone. It was one thing to navigate the bayou, but doing so with what felt like an audience made it more complicated. "So, who's in charge here at the moment?"

"Officer Blayne Guidry's up ahead near where the body is," the officer replied, pointing toward the section of the bayou where the scene had been cordoned off. "He's with the guy who found it."

"I know, Blayne," the deputy nodded. "Worked with him on a few cases before. Solid guy."

"Yeah, he's been holding it down up there. Go ahead—you'll see him at the scene," the Lake Arthur officer said, waving the deputy forward.

They maneuvered their boats carefully toward the body, keeping the engines just above idle to avoid disturbing the murky waters. The sheriff's deputies had come prepared, with three boats in total, one of which carried the coroner to process the body once they arrived at the scene officially. The quiet hum of the motors seemed to echo ominously in the otherwise silent bayou, the weight of the situation palpable as they neared the location.

In the lead boat, Deputy Michael Fruge pulled up alongside Beau's small aluminum vessel. His gaze shifted to Blayne Guidry, standing with his arms crossed and a sad look on his face. The familiarity between the two law enforcement officers was apparent as soon as they made eye contact.

"Hello, Blayne," Michael called out, his voice calm yet carrying the moment's seriousness. "It's been a while since I've seen you."

Blayne nodded, his expression a mix of relief and tension. "Hey, Michael. Yeah, it's been too long."

Blayne turned toward Beau, still sitting in his boat, looking visibly shaken from the morning's events. "Beau Benoit, let me introduce you to Michael Fruge, Deputy with the Vermilion Sheriff's Department."

Still somewhat dazed, Beau quickly nodded and said, "Hello."

"Hello, Beau," Michael replied, acknowledging him with a nod of his own. Then, without missing a beat, he shifted his attention back to the matter at hand. "So, what exactly do we have here? All we were told was that a body had been found in this stretch of the bayou."

Blayne took a breath before starting. "Well, Beau was out here early this morning, doing some fishing. He had a line get snagged on some cypress knees right over there," he said, pointing to the tangled roots sticking out of the water. "When he went to free it—"

Michael cut him off, and his tone suddenly became graver. "Let me guess. You found a woman's naked body floating between those cypress knees?"

Blayne paused, the words catching in his throat. "Um, yes. That's exactly what happened." He blinked, clearly taken aback. "How did you know that if you didn't have the details yet?"

Michael's face hardened, his gaze fixed on the water. "Because we had a similar case a few months back," he said, his voice laced with tension. "Almost identical. Found a woman's body along this same bayou, just closer to Gueydan."

The revelation hit Blayne like a punch to the gut. His mind raced, trying to process the implications. The discovery of one body in the bayou was shocking enough, but the mention of a second case—so similar, so recent—sent a wave of dread through him. His thoughts flashed to the woman floating just a few yards away, her pale skin barely visible between the roots and stumps. Had they just stumbled upon the work of something much darker?

Sitting quietly in the boat, Beau looked between the two men, his face paling even further at the mention of a previous case. "You mean...

there's more?" he asked, his voice barely above a whisper.

Michael gave a solemn nod. "Afraid so. And if this is connected, we might deal with something more complicated than a random accident."

"What do we know about the first incident?" Blayne asked, his brow furrowed in concern. He needed to understand the scope of what they were dealing with, especially if this case was linked to another.

Michael sighed, glancing at the water before answering, "I can't share too many details since the investigation's still active, and honestly, we haven't had any major leads on the case yet."

Blayne nodded, understanding the need for discretion, but he pressed on. "I get that, but what can you tell me? Just the basics — anything that can help us make sense of this."

Michael shifted in the boat, his voice taking on a more serious tone. "The situation was nearly identical, except for how the body was discovered. Two hunters were out with their dogs when the dogs started acting strange, barking and leading them to something unusual. When they checked it out, they found a woman's body floating between the cypress knees, just like this one. Sort of like a cypress tomb."

Blayne glanced at the current scene, the woman's pale body still caught among the stumps. The similarities were unnerving. "And what do we know about the first victim?"

Michael grimaced slightly. "Not a whole lot, unfortunately — just the basics. Her name was Sarah Cormier, age 31, from Crowley, Louisiana. She had blonde hair and blue eyes and was reported missing about two months before we found her body."

Blayne listened closely, mentally filing away the details. Two months missing, he thought. That was a long time for someone to vanish without a trace. "Any signs of foul play with the first girl? Were there indications she'd been… assaulted?"

Michael's expression darkened, his voice lowering as he shared the details. "There were clear signs of abuse. Her wrists and ankles showed marks from being tied up, indicating she was restrained for some time before her death. There was bruising across her back and buttocks, which suggested she'd been beaten or otherwise harmed. And, yeah," he hesitated, his voice becoming more somber, "there were signs of forced entry into the vagina. It was clear she had been violated."

As Michael laid out the grim facts, Blayne felt a chill run through him. He had seen his share of dark cases over the years, but the brutality of this one hit him hard, especially now that it seemed like they were dealing with a possible repeat offender. The thought of another woman, this time the one floating in front of them, having suffered the same fate, made his stomach churn.

"So, the first girl—Sarah Cormier—wasn't just killed," Blayne said, piecing it together out loud. "She was tortured, restrained, assaulted… and then dumped here."

Michael nodded, his jaw tight. "Exactly. And from the looks of it, this case could be heading down the same road, but we won't know until we examine the body."

"This can't be a coincidence," Blayne muttered, shaking his head.

"I agree," Michael said, glancing at the body again. "We might be dealing with someone who knows these waters, someone who's targeting these women and using the bayou to hide their crimes."

Blayne felt a deep sense of urgency welling up inside him. "If this is connected, and it sure seems like it is, we've got a serious problem."

"Agreed," Michael said. "But first, we need to process the body and see exactly what we're dealing with before jumping to conclusions."

Blayne exchanged a look with him, and both men felt the weight of what lay before them. The tension was thick, and they both knew the stakes were high. "We need to handle this scene as if it's part of something much bigger," Blayne said firmly. "We can't afford to overlook anything."

"Absolutely," Michael replied. "Let's get the coroner over here to start documenting everything. Fortunately, the team that worked on the last case is here, so they'll know what to look for and can check for any possible connections."

As the coroner's boat drew closer, Blayne felt an uneasiness settle in the pit of his stomach. There was no shaking the feeling that they had just stumbled into something far darker than any of them anticipated. What had begun as a quiet day of fishing for Beau had swiftly turned into unraveling a mystery that now seemed to have deep, sinister roots lurking in the shadows of the bayou.

The medical team moved with precision, carefully navigating the tangled roots and murky water to photograph the woman's body where it lay among the cypress stumps. The scene was haunting—her pale form half-submerged in the dark waters, eerily still between the ancient roots. Each click of the camera captured the evidence, preserving every angle, every bruise, and every mark. Once they were confident they had documented the scene thoroughly, they carefully pulled the body from the water and into their boat for a closer examination.

The coroner wasted no time, immediately taking the woman's temperature to estimate how long she had been there. "Looks like she's been out here for a few days," the coroner said grimly, making notes in his log. He glanced back at the body, which bore the unmistakable signs of violence and captivity. There were the same marks—wrists and ankles showing the telltale signs of having been tied as if she had been restrained for days. Deep bruises ran along her back and buttocks, a mirror image of the injuries on the body found months earlier.

The unsettling similarities between this victim and the one before her were impossible to ignore. Like Sarah Cormier, this woman was blonde with blue eyes, and though many details were yet to be uncovered, the parallels in the manner of death were becoming undeniable. The team took more photos, methodically capturing every bruise, every contusion, and every detail they could before they transported the body back for a more thorough autopsy.

The coroner, now finished with his initial assessment, approached Michael with an update. His face was stern, lined with disgust at the brutality of what he'd just witnessed. "From what we've seen here, it's almost identical to the first victim. Similar bruising, similar signs of restraint. Both women appear to have been tied up, abused, and left for dead."

Michael's expression darkened as he listened. Though they had little information, it was already too clear that the two cases were connected. He clenched his jaw, irritation, and disgust simmering beneath the surface. It was one thing to deal with a single tragic case, but knowing that this could be the work of a repeat offender, someone who had done this before—and might do it again—was infuriating.

"I don't like where this is headed," Michael muttered under his breath as he glanced over at Blayne, who had been listening intently. Blayne nodded, his expression grim. Both men knew this case was no longer just a tragedy—a pattern and a dangerous one. They were facing something much darker than they had initially anticipated. The women, the locations, the methods—everything pointed to a predator who knew these waters well and had been using the bayou as a place to hide his victims.

The coroner carefully zipped up the body bag, sealing the woman inside with a soft, final sound that seemed to echo in the stillness of the bayou. The medical team moved methodically, packing away their equipment, their faces drawn and serious, knowing the most challenging part of the job wasn't over yet. Navigating back through the crowds of spectators with a body on board would be no easy task. The crowd had only grown since the initial discovery, and the locals' curiosity would undoubtedly make their exit difficult.

Michael turned to Blayne, recognizing the situation at hand. "Blayne, do you think you can help us get escorted back? It will be a mess trying to get through that crowd."

Blayne, who had been quietly observing the coroner's team, nodded. "We'll help you out," he replied. He then turned to Beau, who still sat in his boat, his head in his hands, processing everything that had unfolded.

"Beau, can you give me a ride back to the station?" Blayne asked, his voice gentle.

Beau, still dazed, looked up slowly. "Yeah, I'll take you. I pass the station to return to the boat dock anyway."

Blayne glanced over at the police boats stationed nearby, already thinking ahead. "We'll send two of our boats with you to run interference," he said to Michael, already coordinating a plan. "Did you get everything you need from the area? Because the minute we pull out of here, every spectator will swarm this place."

Michael quickly glanced at his team, which nodded in affirmation. "We've got what we need," he exhaled deeply. Thanks for all the help on this one."

"No problem," Blayne replied. "Just keep us in the loop. Share whatever data you can once you've processed it. We need to stay ahead of this in case anything suspicious that might be related turns up."

Michael's face was set with concern. "As soon as the media gets wind of this, it will be a frenzy. Rumors will fly, and the locals will start talking. You know how it goes."

Blayne nodded. "Exactly why we need to stick close on this one. We'll need facts to reduce the noise between the media storm and local gossip. That's why I asked about sharing info—it helps us find some truth in the chaos."

"You know how it is," Michael said, half-smiling despite the dark circumstances. "We'll share what we can. This case is getting ugly fast."

Blayne picked up his radio and called the police boat stationed closer to the Mermentau River, instructing them to come to their location to help escort the Sheriff's Deputies out of the area. In the meantime, the game wardens would hold the growing crowd of onlookers back, buying them time to clear the scene without unnecessary interruptions or contamination.

As the boats lined up for the ride back, Michael and Blayne exchanged a final glance—a silent acknowledgment of the gravity of the situation. This wasn't over. Not by a long shot.

With a quick nod, Michael and his team moved out, the boats cutting through the water in formation as they returned to town. The body bag in the boat was a grim reminder of the dark reality that lay beneath the surface of this investigation. For Blayne and Michael, both seasoned officers, the sinking feeling in their gut was undeniable. They both knew, deep down, that this was only the beginning of something far more sinister lurking in the shadows of the bayou.

Blayne stood in Beau's boat as the boats disappeared, watching the horizon. The bayou, once a place of calm and solitude, had turned into a place of nightmares. And this wasn't the end—only the start of something darker, something they would all be chasing in the coming days.

## Chapter 9

Leah's heart raced as she lay on the bed, her worst fears slowly becoming a reality. She was still tied up, blindfolded, and gagged, her body restrained in a way that made escape impossible. Every muscle in her body was tense, conflicted between the terror of what was happening and a strange, unwelcome sensation stirring within her. She didn't want to be here, didn't want to be in this situation. But as much as she tried to push the thoughts away, a part of her—the part she didn't understand—was growing louder. It frightened her even more.

The silence in the room was suffocating, and though she couldn't see her captor, she could feel his presence. He was still standing beside her. She could sense his proximity, the weight of his presence making the air feel thick and oppressive. Every instinct in her body told her to be afraid, but the quietness unsettled her even more.

Why isn't he doing anything? she thought. Her mind raced, imagining every possible scenario. The longer he stood there without making a sound, the more terrifying it became. It was as though he was savoring the moment, prolonging her agony, feeding off her fear. She could hear her rapid breathing through her gag, the muffled sound filling her ears as her panic grew.

Leah's thoughts spiraled. What is he waiting for? The anticipation was unbearable. Every second ticked by felt like an eternity, and her mind played tricks on her, conjuring up images of what might come next. She couldn't scream, couldn't move, couldn't plead for him to stop. All she could do was lay there, helpless and vulnerable, waiting for whatever was coming.

Her body tensed as she imagined him watching her, studying her every movement, every breath. The idea that he was standing so close yet not touching her made her skin crawl. The silence felt deliberate, as though he was mentally trying to break her down before making his next move. She strained to listen for any sound, any hint of what he might be doing, but all she could hear was the maddening stillness.

Why isn't he saying anything? she wondered, her mind scrambling for answers. Was he waiting for her to react? Testing her? The uncertainty gnawed at her, intensifying her fear. In her blindness, she had no sense of time—no idea how long she had been lying there, how much time had passed since he had taken her, or what might happen next.

Her body remained frozen in fear and some strange, twisted anticipation. Leah hated herself for it, but there was no denying the conflict brewing inside her. She was terrified, but something about the powerlessness struck a chord deep inside her, a feeling she didn't want to acknowledge. The line between fear and desire was blurring, and it horrified her that she could even feel this way.

But as she lay there, waiting, the uncertainty grew unbearable. She wanted to scream, to demand to know what he was doing and why he wasn't speaking. The silence was driving her mad and amplifying her vulnerability.

Then, without warning, he made his move. Leah felt her body being shifted, rolled onto her left side with deliberate slowness, as though he was savoring the control he had over her. Every nerve in her body was on high alert as she felt the pressure on her arms shift. He was behind her now, and she could feel him messing with the ropes around her wrists. Her heart raced—Was he untying her?

Could this be my chance? Leah's mind screamed. Her thoughts collided, one part filled with panic, the other calculating her next move. If he loosened the ropes, even slightly, she might be able to fight back, strike him, and maybe catch him off guard. He wasn't expecting her to resist—he had no reason to. He likely thought she was too afraid, too broken by this point, to try anything. But if she could get her right arm free, she could swing, aim for his face, maybe his throat, something, anything that would hinder him long enough for her to escape.

She played the scenario over in her mind, a plan forming in the chaos. If I strike, I have to do it fast, and I have to hit hard. Her wrists felt raw from the ropes, her body sore from being restrained, but adrenaline surged through her veins. She could feel him working the ropes, and her heartbeat quickened with each slight tug. Just a little more… she thought. Just let my hands be free…

But then, doubt crept in. She was lying on her left side, meaning her only option was to swing with her right arm. The angle could have been more comfortable, and the leverage could have been better. Could she even land a hit hard enough to hurt him, or would it only provoke him? What if she missed? What if the blow was too weak? What if her attempt to escape backfired and only enraged him?

Her mind was racing, her thoughts tangled with fear and determination. She remembered the smack he had given her before, the sharp sting on her hip as a warning. That had been for something small, just for not releasing his hand. What would he do if she tried to hurt him? The thought made her stomach turn. Would he do more than smack her? Would he hurt her in ways she couldn't imagine? The fear of the unknown consequences froze her momentarily, the weight of the decision pressing down on her.

What if this is my only chance to escape? The thought burned in her mind, but so did the fear of failure. She could already feel the consequences of missing, of not striking hard enough, playing out in her head. Would he lash out in anger? Would the punishment be more than a stinging slap?

Her body tensed, her muscles coiled as if ready to strike, but her mind was paralyzed by indecision. She imagined herself swinging wildly, desperate, hoping to land a blow that would cripple him, but the other side of her mind whispered warnings—What if it's not enough? What if this makes it worse?

The ropes around her wrists shifted again, and she felt the slack. The moment of decision was coming. Her breathing quickened, and her heart thundered in her chest. Do I strike? Do I wait? Every second seemed to stretch out, time slowing as she weighed her options. Her survival instincts screamed at her to fight, to take the risk. But fear… fear of what would happen if she failed—gnawed at her equally.

Her captor remained silent, his movements careful, deliberate. Whatever he was planning, she knew she didn't have much time to decide. This could be her only chance, she thought once more, her mind flickering between courage and terror.

With no time to waste, Leah made up her mind—she would take her chance to escape. She didn't care about the consequences if she failed. Every fiber of her being told her that this might be her only opportunity. She lay there, her body tense with anticipation, waiting for the ropes around her wrists to loosen. The fear that had paralyzed her moments ago was replaced by a singular focus—fight.

She could feel him working on the knots, the ropes slightly loosening, the sensation of the rough material no longer biting into her skin as much. Just a little more, she thought, her breath quickening. She had already decided that when her arms were free, she would swing with everything she had, aiming for any vital spot she could reach—his face, his throat—anything that would stun him long enough for her to break free. Her heart pounded in her chest as the ropes became looser, and the seconds felt like hours as she prepared to strike.

Then, she felt it. The moment she had been waiting for—the rope around her wrists was no longer holding them together. This is it, she thought. She rolled back on her back, and her arms shot up without hesitation, aiming for a decisive blow in his direction. She didn't know—she couldn't afford to. Her body moved purely on instinct, fueled by fear, rage, and desperation.

But she realized something was wrong when her arms flew into the air in a split second. Instead of the freedom she expected, her arms were suddenly pulled taut and restrained above her head. Her heart sank as the awful realization hit her. He anticipated this.

Her captor had outsmarted her. While she had been focusing on the ropes around her wrists, he must have silently tied additional restraints to her hands, securing them to the headboard while he worked to free them from each other. She hadn't noticed until it was too late, and now, instead of her wrists being bound together, her arms were tied above her head, leaving her even more exposed and vulnerable than before.

Panic surged through her as she tested the restraints, yanking her arms downward with all her might. But the ropes held firm, and no struggle could free her now. She had lost her one chance—the only moment she had planned so carefully for—and he had been ready for it all along. Her mind screamed with frustration and fear, her body trembling as the weight of her situation crashed over her.

She had failed. The swing she had hoped would deliver her from this nightmare had been in vain, and now she was even more helpless than before. Her captor hadn't said a word, but his silence was deafening. He had known what she would do and had prepared for it.

Leah could feel her captor's presence shift as he moved from where her arms were tied to the ropes, constraining her ankles. Her mind was still reeling from her failed attempt to escape, but she couldn't help but focus on what was coming next. She knew there was no chance of kicking her legs free once they were untied—he was too careful, too calculated. He had already anticipated her arm attempt, and she was sure he wouldn't give her any opportunity to fight back with her legs.

Her suspicions were confirmed as she felt the tension in the ropes around her ankles begin to ease. But even before the bindings were entirely undone, she felt the pull—the slow, deliberate separation of her legs. Her captor wasn't just untying her ankles; he was already spreading her legs apart, pulling them into position. The looser the ropes became, the wider her legs were spread.

A fresh wave of panic surged through her body. She couldn't stop or fight it, and the realization made her feel even more helpless. The ropes that had once kept her bound together were now gone, but instead of granting her freedom, they had only left her more exposed. She lay there, her arms restrained above her head, her legs pulled apart, and her body completely vulnerable.

The thin fabric of her sundress offered little comfort. It clung to her body, a fragile barrier between her and whatever was coming. The room seemed colder now, though she couldn't tell if it was from the air or the dread pooling in her chest. Her breath came in short, shaky gasps, and she tried to prepare herself mentally for what might come next, but no bracing could stop the fear from creeping in.

Without warning, Leah felt herself being flipped onto her stomach, the sudden shift in position catching her completely off guard. Her heart pounded wildly as she lay there, her arms still tied above her head, and her legs now adjusted into an even more vulnerable position. Every nerve in her body was alight with fear, the tension unbearable as she anticipated his next move.

His hand's cold, calculating touch began tracing its way up her left leg, starting at her ankle and slowly moving higher, sending shivers of dread coursing through her. She squeezed her eyes shut, trying to block out the sensation, but it was impossible. Each touch felt deliberate, each moment drawn out to amplify her terror. When his hand reached the hem of her sundress, the last barrier between her skin and the oppressive darkness of this situation, she braced herself, clenching her muscles in fear.

Then, she heard it—a sound she had dreaded since she'd been tied up. The unmistakable, chilling snip of scissors cutting through fabric. Her heart sank as the realization of what was happening hit her. He's removing my dress, she thought in horror. The dress, the only thing shielding her body, was being taken from her with each deliberate cut.

With each snip of the scissors, the panic in her chest grew heavier. She could feel the cold metal blades of the scissors grazing against her skin, cutting through the thin fabric of her dress. The sensation was unbearable—each touch of the blade a cruel reminder of how powerless she was, how wholly exposed she would soon be. She fought the urge to struggle, knowing it was futile. The ropes around her wrists and the position of her legs left her with no chance to resist.

The fabric peeled away as he cut higher and higher, the dress slowly falling apart with each slice. The cool air hit her skin as more of her body became exposed. She could feel the cold metal against her buttocks, then trailing up her spine as he continued cutting. The vulnerability of being entirely at his mercy left her trembling with fear, her breaths shallow and quick as she waited for the inevitable.

Once he reached the top of the dress, she felt the scissors against her shoulders. The tiny straps that had once held the dress in place were no match for the sharp blades. One by one, they were cut away, the dress now nothing more than a heap of loose fabric barely clinging to her. With a deliberate pull, he removed the dress entirely, leaving her completely exposed, her body trembling as she lay bare before him.

Leah's mind raced with thoughts of what would come next, and her worst fears were fully realized. The feeling of helplessness was suffocating—her body was no longer her own, and she was at the mercy of her captor. Her nakedness made her feel even more vulnerable, her skin prickling with a mix of fear and shame.

The silence around her was maddening, each second stretching out, thick with tension. The sound of the scissors still echoed in her mind, the way they had sliced through the thin fabric of her sundress, leaving her completely exposed. That final, tangible barrier between her and her captor had been stripped away, leaving her skin naked and unprotected. Now, she only had the crushing weight of fear and the sickening anticipation of what would come next.

Then, without warning, she felt it—a sudden, sharp pain slicing through the silence. The impact was startling, and before her mind could fully process what had happened, the sound followed—the unmistakable crack of a paddle hitting her bare skin. The pain surged across her buttocks, spreading a searing heat that pulsed with every heartbeat.

## Chapter 10

Michael Fruge found himself navigating the murky waters of Bayou Queue De Tortue again, a familiar but unwelcome setting. The call had come in early that morning, and from the moment he heard it, a sinking feeling settled in his gut. Another body had been found—another woman, naked and floating between the twisted cypress stumps. It was the same grim scenario he had faced twice before, and as his boat cut through the still waters of the swamp, he couldn't shake the heavy sense of déjà vu.

This time, the body had been discovered roughly midway between the first two locations. The pattern was becoming more apparent now—whoever was behind these horrifying acts seemed to be using this specific stretch of the bayou as their personal dumping ground. With its isolated, maze-like waterways and dense cypress trees, the swamp offered a kind of natural cover that swallowed evidence, making it a perfect hiding place for someone who knew the area well.

Michael's grip tightened on the steering wheel as he guided his boat through the winding channels. The deceptive quiet of the bayou, once a place of solace, now felt menacing, as if the water held secrets too dark to acknowledge. The thought of yet another victim—another life cut short and discarded like trash—pressed heavily on him. This case was no longer just a tragic mystery. It was evolving into something far more sinister, something that pointed toward the terrifying prospect of a serial killer at work lurking in the shadows of the bayou.

But why? There was always a reason, even if it was buried deep in the twisted mind of the killer. Michael's frustration gnawed at him as he thought of the lost lives, the grieving families, and the creeping fear that had taken hold of the small communities along the bayou. Every time a new body was found, it sent shock waves through the area. People were beginning to whisper about the "Bayou Butcher," a name locals had given the faceless monster stalking their waters.

As he neared the location where the latest body had been discovered, Michael slowed the boat. The cypress trees loomed overhead, their gnarled roots snaking into the water like skeletal hands. The scene ahead was painfully familiar—another woman's body, eerily still, caught between the stumps as if the swamp itself had swallowed her whole.

Bringing the boat to a stop, Michael reached for his radio, its familiar weight in his hand offering little comfort. "I'm here," he said, his voice steady despite the tension tightening in his chest. "Another one. Same as the last two." The words felt thick and bitter on his tongue, like something sour he couldn't quite spit out. Each time he had to utter those words, it was as if they dug deeper into his soul, and the question that haunted him every time was how many more times he would have to say them.

He paused for a moment, glancing over to where the body had been found. It was an all too familiar sight—the woman's blonde hair drifting on the surface of the water, her lifeless body floating between the cypress stumps, carried ever so slightly by the gentle ripples of the bayou. The image struck him hard, even though he'd seen it before. This scene, like the others, seemed almost choreographed in its brutality, a macabre display that echoed the horror of the previous two victims. If it weren't for the slight differences in the terrain, he could almost believe he was staring at the same body as before.

Michael took a deep breath, forcing himself to focus. He reached into his pocket, pulling out his notepad and pen, ready to document the details before the rest of the team arrived. He needed to get down everything he could before the scene became crowded before the inevitable hum of investigators, deputies, and coroner officials filled the swamp with chatter. He scribbled notes—blonde hair, naked body, positioned between the stumps—his mind racing for some hidden clue, some overlooked detail that could finally lead them to the killer.

Maybe this time, he thought, this will be the scene where we find something—a clue, a piece of evidence that finally gives us a lead. He knew they were running out of time. The town was already gripped with fear, and fear could turn dangerous in a place like this. Sooner or later, if they didn't make an arrest, people would start taking matters into their own hands. And the last thing they needed was vigilantes stirring up more trouble in the swamp.

As he continued writing, the faint sound of a boat's engine reached his ears, growing louder with each passing moment. Michael didn't look up right away, assuming it was the other deputies arriving with the coroner. He stayed focused, jotting down everything he could remember—the body's position, the proximity to the different scenes, the slight changes in the environment.

But when the boat came closer, something made him pause. The engine's hum wasn't the same as the sheriff's boats, nor did it sound like the motor on the coroner's vessel. Michael finally looked up from his notepad, squinting toward the source of the sound. His brow furrowed as he saw a familiar face coming into view. It wasn't the team he had been expecting.

It was Blayne Guidry pulling up in a Lake Arthur Police Boat.

The sight of Blayne caught Michael off guard. He hadn't called Blayne in for this, and Blayne wasn't typically part of these investigations. In the middle of a crime scene, his presence here was unexpected and raised questions. What was Blayne doing out here? Had he heard something? Or had the rumors of another body spread so quickly through town that even Blayne couldn't resist coming out to see for himself?

Michael stood up in the boat, waiting as Blayne pulled closer. His gut told him that this was going to complicate things. Blayne had a way of digging into matters and inserting himself into situations where his curiosity sometimes got the better. As Blayne's boat came up alongside Michael's, the air between them was thick with unspoken tension, the weight of another murder hanging heavy in the swamp.

"Hey Blayne, what are you doing way out here?" Michael asked, raising an eyebrow as Blayne's boat eased closer.

"I just happened to be out here patrolling the area when I heard the call come across the radio that another body had been found," Blayne replied, his tone casual. Still, Michael could see the curiosity burning in his eyes.

"Patrolling?" Michael questioned, his voice sharp. "This area is outside your jurisdiction, don't you think?"

Blayne gave a slight shrug, not quite apologetic. "I know, but the curiosity got the better of me. Ever since the last body was found, and you said it was the second one, I had this feeling there'd be a third. I couldn't shake it."

Michael sighed, glancing over his shoulder toward the still waters where the woman's body floated. "Well, it appears your instincts were right. The third one showed up."

Blayne leaned forward, trying to get a better look past Michael. "Same scenario?"

Michael nodded grimly. "From what I can tell, it's the same story. Blonde hair, naked, floating between the cypress knees." He paused for a moment, the weight of the repetition bearing down on him. "It's all too familiar."

Blayne's face tightened, and he furrowed his brow. "Did you find anything in the last case that gets you closer to solving this? Anything new?"

"Not much more than what you'd find in the paper," Michael replied, the frustration creeping into his voice. "Her name was Rebecca Boudreaux, from Estherwood. She worked at a local law firm. That's all we've got. The only connection so far is that both victims had blonde hair and blue eyes."

Michael's gaze shifted back to the water, where the third victim lay, eerily still. "And judging by the hair color we can see here, it looks like this one fits the same pattern."

Blayne frowned, his eyes narrowing as he looked at the body in the distance. "That's it? Just hair color and eye color? No connections between their jobs, their social circles, anything else?"

Michael shook his head. "Nothing concrete yet. We're digging through everything—family, friends, work connections—but so far, nothing sticks. No common link other than their appearance."

Blayne's lips pressed into a thin line, and for a moment, the air between them was thick with unspoken questions. The same frustration that gnawed at Michael was written across Blayne's face. A string of murders with no apparent motive, no solid leads—it was the kind of case that wore down even the most seasoned officers. And the more bodies that turned up, the more desperate the situation became.

"I keep thinking," Blayne started, breaking the silence, "about how these bodies are all being found out here. Why this area? It's like the killer knows this place, knows the bayou."

Michael nodded, his thoughts echoing Blayne's. "Yeah, that's been bothering me too. Whoever's doing this knows how to navigate these waters. This part of the bayou isn't just some random spot—it's deliberate."

Blayne's eyes flicked back to Michael. "Then the question is, why here? What's so special about this area?"

Michael sighed, his frustration deepening. "That's what we need to figure out. There's a reason they keep dumping bodies in this stretch of the bayou, but so far, we've got no answers."

The two men stood silently for a moment, the swamp around them unnervingly still as if even the bayou held its breath. The weight of the unsolved murders hung heavily between them, and they both knew that with each passing day, the chances of catching the killer slipped further and further away. Time was running out, and neither could ignore that grim reality.

As they stood contemplating the grimness of the situation, the faint hum of approaching boats broke the silence. Michael and Blayne turned toward the sound and saw the Sheriff's boats coming into view, cutting through the misty waters. The first boat carried the deputies, while the second had the coroner and medical staff. The scene was becoming all too familiar—boats arriving, officers setting up a perimeter, the slow, methodical process of recovering yet another body.

Without much thought, Michael motioned the deputies toward the body's location. "Over there," he gestured, his tone distant. His mind was still focused on the conversation with Blayne. His attention lingered on the team as they got to work, documenting the scene as they had done twice. Everything was following the same routine, and that was starting to worry Michael.

Routine often bred complacency, which was dangerous in cases like this. The team was good at their job—thorough and professional—but Michael couldn't shake the feeling that the sheer repetition of the process might lead to mistakes. The thought gnawed at him as he and

Blayne continued watching from a distance, observing the coroner's team record every detail, collect evidence, and prepare the body for transport.

"This is starting to become too much of a routine," Michael muttered, his voice tinged with frustration. He knew routine could dull the senses and make people go through the motions instead of staying sharp. And right now, they couldn't afford to miss anything.

Blayne nodded in agreement. "You're right. It's like we're on autopilot, just waiting for the next one to appear. But what happens if we miss something? That's how killers keep getting away."

Michael's mind was racing, thinking about the scene before them and the two cases that had preceded it. They couldn't afford to miss even the slightest clue. They were desperate for a break—anything that could lead them to the person responsible for these horrific murders. Every step had to be meticulous, and there was no room for error.

"We need a break," Michael said, his voice low but filled with urgency. "We need something. A clue, a lead—anything that can give us some direction."

Blayne glanced at him, sensing the frustration building. "It'll come," he said, though even he didn't sound convinced. "It has to. We need to stay on top of this."

Michael didn't respond, his eyes fixed on the team working near the water's edge. He knew they were doing everything by the book, but his fear of complacency lingered. The killer had slipped through their fingers twice already. If they missed something now, there might be a fourth victim. And that was a reality neither of them could stomach.

Michael watched grimly as the coroner's team zipped the lifeless body into another body bag, a task that had become disturbingly routine. He could see the coroner motioning to speak with him, so Michael steered his boat over, easing it beside the coroner's so they could converse without yelling across the bayou. The eerie stillness of the swamp pressed down on them, amplifying every tiny sound, every quiet exchange.

The coroner's face was grim as he spoke. "Looks the same as the other two," he said, his voice flat with the weight of repetition. "Blonde hair, blue eyes, bound marks at the wrists and feet—same as before."

Michael sighed, his eyes narrowing as he glanced at the bag holding another victim. "Yeah, based on how the body was found, I figured you'd say that," he muttered, his frustration evident. He hesitated for a second before asking, "Was there anything else? Something that might have been a little different this time?"

The coroner shook his head, his expression apologetic. "Not from the actual crime scene. Everything's consistent with the first two. But I might find something once I get the body back to the lab and can do a thorough examination. Sometimes, things don't show up until we look closer."

Michael clenched his jaw, feeling the weight of disappointment settle in his chest. "Thanks, Doc," he said, trying to mask the frustration in his tone. "I was just hoping the killer might've slipped up, left something—anything we could use to get a lead."

The coroner nodded sympathetically. "I get it. We're all hoping for something. I'll let you know when I've got my report ready. Maybe there's something we're missing."

Michael gave a half-hearted nod and watched as the coroner's boat began preparing to leave. The conversation had confirmed what he feared—nothing had changed except the number of victims. There was still no new clue, no break in the case, nothing to give them any leads. He was painfully aware that if they didn't figure something out soon, it was only a matter of time before they found another body.

He returned to where Blayne was waiting, his frustration palpable. "Coroner says it's just like the others. It has the same cause of death and the same signs of restraint—no new clues at the scene," Michael said, his voice tight with irritation.

Blayne listened, his face reflecting the same concern. He knew Michael was feeling the weight of this case more than anyone, and with each new victim, the pressure was mounting. "It's like the killer's taunting us," Blayne remarked quietly. "Each time, the same method, the same area. It's like they know we can't get ahead of them."

Michael nodded, his brow furrowed. "Yeah, and that's what's driving me crazy. They're smart—too smart. They know these waters and know how to hide evidence. But we have to catch a break at some point."

Blayne could see the exhaustion in Michael's eyes, the heavy burden of responsibility weighing him down. "We'll figure this out," Blayne said, though his tone lacked the confidence he wanted to project.

"There's always something they miss."

Michael didn't respond, his mind racing ahead, anticipating the next body they would inevitably find if things didn't change. He hated the feeling of being two steps behind, of knowing there was a killer out there, slipping through their grasp with each murder.

After their conversation, everyone began preparing to leave. The coroner and deputies packed up their equipment, the somber mood hanging over the team like a dark cloud. Three sheriff's boats moved in one direction, heading back toward the station, the scene's weight behind them. Blayne gave Michael a final nod before heading in the opposite direction, back toward Lake Arthur. Even as their boats parted ways, the tension between them remained unspoken—an acknowledgment that, despite their efforts, the killer had gotten away with another murder.

As Michael headed from the crime scene, he stared at the water, the frustration building in his chest. They had nothing: no new leads, clues, just another victim to add to the growing count. And deep down, Michael knew that unless something changed, there would be a fourth and then a fifth. The killer wouldn't stop until they made a mistake—or until he did.

# *Chapter 11*

Leah gasped involuntarily, her breath strangled behind the gag as the sharp sting of the paddle cracked across her bare skin. The force of the strike sent shockwaves through her body, her muscles instinctively clenching to recoil, to move, to escape the pain—but the restraints held her firm. She couldn't move, couldn't twist away. The ropes binding her wrists and ankles dug into her skin, a harsh reminder of her powerlessness, leaving her completely exposed and vulnerable to whatever her captor had planned.

Panic surged through her chest, her heartbeat pounding in her ears as she tried to process what was happening. The sting from the paddle burned across her buttocks, the pain fresh and biting. Her mind raced, grasping for anything to help her make sense of the moment. But the sharpness of the pain refused to let her think clearly, grounding her in the brutal reality of her helplessness.

Before recovering from the first strike, she felt the second one, harder and more deliberate. The paddle connected with the same tender spot, and Leah's body tensed up in response, her muscles locking as a surge of pain jolted through her. She wanted to scream, to cry out, but the gag in her mouth muffled every sound, leaving her voiceless, trapped in her suffering.

The second blow was worse than the first. The area, already throbbing and tender, magnified the sensation, sending a searing, burning ache through her. The sting of the paddle radiated throughout her body, her buttocks now raw and sensitive to the slightest touch. The pain lingered, pulsating with every breath she took, leaving her gasping for air behind the gag. She felt like her skin was on fire, the burning sensation refusing to subside.

Bound tightly, she couldn't reach the places that ached. Her wrists were pinned above her head, her ankles secured, and she was entirely at her captor's mercy. The thought made her heart race even faster, fear mixing with the physical pain, creating a whirlwind of emotions that she couldn't escape. She couldn't even anticipate when the next strike would come, her body locked in constant tension as she waited for the paddle to land again.

Leah's mind was a chaotic mess of terror, pain, and confusion. She couldn't fathom why this was happening, why she had been chosen for this cruel torment, and each second that passed stretched into an eternity, the pain radiating from her buttocks up through her spine, leaving her breathless. The cold air of the room felt cruel against her exposed skin, only amplifying the sharp contrast of the burning pain.

Leah braced herself for the next strike of the paddle, her body already tensed, muscles clenched in preparation for the expected pain. Every nerve in her lower body was still raw from the previous blows, her mind trying to steel itself for the next inevitable strike. But instead of the sharp crack of the paddle across her already sensitive buttocks, a different sensation suddenly shot across her skin—a sting that was somehow worse, spreading broader and more unexpected.

The leather straps came down hard across her back, catching her completely off guard. The sudden bite of the straps, lashing across her skin, sent shockwaves of pain through her body. Leah gasped behind the gag, her whole body convulsing as she tried to cope with the new level of pain. She had prepared herself mentally for the familiar sting of the paddle, but this—this was something entirely different. The multiple strands of leather whipped across her skin with a viciousness that made her back arch involuntarily in response, her body straining against the restraints as if trying to escape the burn.

The leather straps cut across her back in quick succession, the pain spreading like wildfire as they struck in different places, each one delivering a sting that left her breathless. The sudden change in her captor's method of torture left her reeling, her mind scrambling to catch up with the onslaught of sensations. It wasn't just the sting—it was the unpredictability of where the straps would land next, the agony of not knowing when or where the pain would strike again. The randomness of the blows felt like a cruel game, one she had no control over.

She couldn't scream, beg, or even make a sound that might signal her distress. The gag in her mouth held her silent, the only noises in the room being the whip-like crack of the straps and her muffled gasps for breath. The sound of leather cutting through the air before it met her flesh was terrifying—it was the only warning she got, but it wasn't enough.

Leah's body shook with the intensity of the pain. Her mind was a whirlwind of panic and suffering, unable to process what was happening quickly enough. The pain was too much, too intense, and too relentless. She felt herself losing the battle to stay in control. Every part of her wanted to thrash, to fight back, to break free from the restraints, but there was no point. She was entirely at his mercy, unable to stop the torment that was raining down on her from every angle.

As Leah braced herself for another punishing blow, her body tensed in anticipation. But instead of the sharp sting of leather or the harsh slap of the paddle, she felt something completely different—something soft, delicate, and unexpected. The contrast was so sudden that her body reacted instinctively, her muscles flexing in surprise as the sensation rippled across her skin.

It was as if a light, teasing feather was being drawn across the very spots where the pain had once dominated. The areas that the brutal strikes of the paddle had tortured and the straps were now alive with a new sensation, the gentleness of the feather somehow heightening the sensitivity that still lingered. Her body trembled under the touch, not knowing how to process this change from violence to something far more sensual.

Her captor dragged the feather down her back, starting on the left side, barely grazing her skin. It was maddeningly light, but every inch of her body responded as if electrified. The feather trailed along the curve of her spine, sliding lower until it reached her buttocks, where the pain was still raw from the paddling. The soft touch against such sensitive skin was almost unbearable. The sensation was not one of pain, but it was intense all the same—her mind and body reeling from the shift in sensations.

Leah could feel the feather tracing the back of her thigh, and she squirmed involuntarily, her muscles tightening and relaxing in response to the touch. She couldn't escape it—the ropes still held her firmly in place—but the contrast between pain and softness was dizzying. The feather reached down to her foot, and the sensation was almost ticklish for a moment, but then it changed again.

As the feather was slowly drawn back up, this time along the inside of her leg, a fresh wave of sensation spread through her. It was maddening how gentle it was, yet it felt like every nerve in her body was on fire. When the feather reached her inner thigh, just past her knee, her breathing became shallow, each breath catching in her throat. She didn't know how to react. Her body, still recovering from the pain, now responded to this new stimulus with an intensity she hadn't expected.

Then, the feather moved higher, brushing against her upper thigh's soft, vulnerable skin, inching closer to the most sensitive part of her body. Leah's entire being tensed as it grazed her inner thigh, sending a shiver up her spine. Her captor continued with deliberate slowness, letting the feather trail along the delicate area between her legs, running it straight across her vagina, the lightest touch yet the most overwhelming.

Leah's body convulsed as the feather moved across her, her breath catching in her throat. The feeling wasn't painful but so intense that she couldn't stop herself from reacting. The feather traveled up the center of her buttocks, brushing against the raw, sensitive skin where she had been struck before, causing her to arch involuntarily. Her body, still aching from the previous abuse, was now alive with an overwhelming mix of sensations—pain, yes, but also something more profound, more confusing.

Her mind spun, trying to reconcile the conflicting emotions surging through her. The pain that had dominated her thoughts was now interwoven with something else—something sensual, even arousing. The soft touch of the feather against her most intimate and vulnerable parts sent waves of heat through her body, mingling with the remnants of pain in a way she couldn't control. She convulsed again, not out of fear or resistance this time, but because the feelings had become too much to bear.

Leah's thoughts were a whirlwind of confusion. Her body betrayed her, responding to the touch in ways she didn't understand. The feather's teasing strokes, once a relief from pain, now stirred something more profound within her. Every nerve in her body seemed to be on fire, and yet, it wasn't agony—it was an emotion she didn't want to feel but couldn't stop.

He traced the feather lightly, teasingly, down the curve of Leah's lower back, brushing it against her buttocks and grazing her inner thighs. Her breath hitched, her body responding to the soft, irresistible touch even though she fought against the rising tide of sensation. Every gentle sweep of the feather heightened her awareness; every flick made her pulse quicken, betraying her resolve.

The feather slid down the inside of her right leg, barely skimming her skin, and Leah shivered involuntarily. The sensation lingered like a ghost, the delicate caress tormenting her with its softness. As it neared her ankle, she clenched her hands, the struggle within her intensifying. But before she could prepare herself, the feather traveled back up—slowly, sensuously—gliding behind her knee, where she tensed, the touch too light to resist, too overwhelming to ignore.

Her thighs quivered when the feather reached the sensitive curve of her backside. The lingering pain from earlier punishments mixed with the unexpected softness of the feather's stroke created a confusing rush of emotions—pain, and pleasure collided in a raw, primal response she couldn't control. Her body shook, betraying her, and she gasped as her nerves fired, every inch of her skin alive with sensation.

He paused, savoring the sight of her vulnerability, before continuing the deliberate torture. The feather trailed over the welts left by the leather straps, and the sharp contrast of pain and pleasure set her nerves ablaze. The intensity surged, tightening her body as it twisted beneath the sensations. Her chest heaved with shallow, ragged breaths, her nipples hardening, her pulse pounding.

When the feather reached her spine, it descended slowly— agonizingly slowly—along the length of her back. Leah's body arched, craving and dreading the touch all at once. The soft plume slid lower, brushing over her buttocks again before dipping between her thighs, stroking her in the most intimate place. The lightness of the touch was maddening. Her legs trembled as wetness bloomed between them, a sign of her body's submission, a betrayal of her mind's resistance.

She clenched her jaw, trying to stifle the moans rising in her throat, but her body was no longer hers to command. His movements' slow, deliberate pace drove her to the brink, and though she fought against the flood of desire, it was overwhelming and relentless. She could feel herself spiraling, her defenses eroding as the pleasure built to a crescendo.

He repeated the process—repeatedly—each time, driving her closer to an edge she didn't want to fall over. The feather moved in that same excruciatingly slow pattern, tracing the familiar paths and igniting the same unbearable sensations. Her body trembled under the onslaught, torn between resistance and surrender, pleasure and torment.

By the time he reached her back for the third time, she could barely keep still, her body begging for more even as her mind screamed for release. She was trapped in a whirlwind of sensation, her desire stoked to a fever pitch, with no escape from the pleasure that consumed her.

Her body responded with a mind of its own, slick with arousal, her every nerve on fire. The feather was both a curse and a blessing—a reminder of his power over her and a release of the control she no longer possessed. Each stroke heightened her agony and her ecstasy, drawing her deeper into the sensations she couldn't deny. She was at his mercy, and there was no way out but through.

As Leah braced herself for the familiar touch of the feather, her skin was hypersensitive from the prior teasing, and something different pressed against her. It was firmer than the feather, a new sensation that sent a jolt of anticipation through her already trembling body. She inhaled sharply as he placed it between her legs, letting the unfamiliar object glide against her swollen, wet lips. The soft, deliberate movements up and down her slit heightened the tension, teasing her in ways that left her on the verge of unraveling.

Her breath quickened as it passed over her clitoris, the light, teasing friction causing her legs to tremble, her hips shifting involuntarily toward the source of her desire. He dragged the object down again, sliding between her most sensitive spots, just brushing the surface, tormenting her with each stroke. The pressure was perfect, leaving her aching for more, her arousal already pooling between her thighs.

Then, without warning, everything changed.

A slow, steady vibration began as though her entire world had shifted. The device buzzed to life against her clit, and Leah gasped, her breath catching in her throat. The sensation was intense—electric— and sent ripples of pleasure through her entire body. Her nerves were already frayed from the feather's earlier torment, and this sudden, throbbing pressure against her most sensitive spot tipped her over the edge faster than she could comprehend.

In seconds, her body betrayed her ultimately.

The orgasm crashed over her, sudden and overwhelming, seizing her in its grip. She cried out, her voice strangled by the sheer intensity of the release. Her muscles clenched as waves of ecstasy tore through her. The convulsions were uncontrollable—her legs shaking, her hands bound above her head, as her body writhed, lost in the pleasure that consumed her.

It felt like the world had collapsed around her, and all that existed was the blinding pleasure wrapping her frame. She had never felt anything like this before, the intensity magnified by the feather's earlier caress and the relentless vibration now focused on her throbbing clit. It wasn't just an orgasm; it was an eruption of sensation that shattered every wall she had left.

Her breath came in ragged gasps, her chest heaving as her body convulsed with each wave of release. She tried to control it, to stop the quaking of her limbs, but it was impossible. The pleasure was too intense, too raw. Every nerve in her body felt like it was on fire, lit up by the continuous vibrations that he kept pressing against her, prolonging the orgasm, keeping her teetering on the edge of insanity.

She tried to clamp her thighs around the object as if trying to escape the unbearable pleasure, but the sensation only heightened, pulling her deeper into the intoxicating rush. Her moans filled the air, desperate and unrestrained, her body no longer hers to command.

She felt like she was being torn apart, the climax stretching on, refusing to release her from its hold. Each tremor felt like a new wave of bliss, and though her mind screamed for a reprieve, her body craved more. She was lost in it, consumed by a profound pleasure that felt almost unreal. Time seemed to blur, and she couldn't tell if the orgasm had lasted seconds or minutes, only that it left her shattered, trembling, and yearning for more.

Her breathing was erratic, her body still buzzing with aftershocks, the throbbing between her legs relentless. Even as the vibrations subsided, the memory of them lingered, the ache of pleasure still pulsing in her core. She felt raw, exposed, utterly vulnerable—and yet, all she wanted was to feel it again. The hunger inside her was insatiable, her body trembling from the force of the release but aching for another touch, another sensation to tip her over the edge once more.

She had never been pushed this far, never felt so entirely at the mercy of her own body. And yet, in that vulnerability, something was intoxicating, making her want to surrender to the overwhelming sensation all over again.

## Chapter 12

Leah's breath came in sharp, uneven gasps, her chest rising and falling as her body trembled with the aftershocks of the orgasm. Every muscle felt taut, her nerves still buzzing from the intensity of the release. Her legs shook uncontrollably, the lingering waves of pleasure making her entire body convulse, sending jolts of sensation rippling through her. The line between pleasure and distress blurred, her mind unable to distinguish whether she was overwhelmed by ecstasy or something far more primal. Her body's reaction was so raw, so intense, it left her teetering between the two.

Then, without warning, he grabbed her and flipped her onto her back. The sudden movement made her gasp, her bound body helpless to resist as she was repositioned. The moment her bare skin touched the sheets, the stinging reminder of her earlier paddling flared up. The rough fabric rubbed against the welts on her backside and thighs, reigniting the fiery sensation of her punished flesh. The sheets clung to her sweat-slick skin, amplifying the sting, making it sharper, more unbearable. It was as if her body was caught in a whirlwind of sensations—pleasure and pain weaving together into something she couldn't escape.

Her back arched involuntarily as the sensations hit her all at once—the soreness, the rawness, and the lingering pleasure from her orgasm blending into one overwhelming experience. Her nipples, still hard and aching, grazed the sheets as her body writhed, each movement only intensifying the friction. Deep wetness pooled between her legs, the evidence of her pleasure staining the bed beneath her, a visible mark of the helpless arousal she could no longer control.

Leah's entire body felt like it was on fire, every nerve ending sparking with sensitivity. The simple touch of the sheets against her battered skin sent her into another wave of uncontrollable shaking. The overstimulation was maddening. The orgasm hadn't faded, and now, the lingering tremors were only heightened by the fabric's rough texture. She felt her muscles tensing again, her body caught in a loop of sensation she hadn't anticipated. Her thighs clenched together, her hips shifting restlessly against the sheets as the aftershocks kept rolling through her, each one more intense than the last.

She hadn't expected this. She hadn't known her body could react this way—so raw, vulnerable, and entirely at the mercy of sensation. Her hands, still bound, twitched uselessly as if they might find some way to ground her to stop the relentless onslaught of feelings. Her mind raced, trying to make sense of it all, but the blindfold and gag kept her trapped in a world of darkness and silence, cut off from any sense of control or understanding.

She felt utterly exposed, the glistening sweat on her skin catching the dim light as she lay there, trembling in the aftermath. Her chest heaved, her breathing still ragged, as if she couldn't draw in enough air. She could feel the wetness between her legs, the evidence of how thoroughly he had undone her, and it only made the shame and desire swirl even deeper inside her. She didn't know how to reconcile what she was feeling—whether to revel in the pleasure or shrink from the fact that she had been pushed so far, so quickly.

Leah's mind swirled with confusion. The blindfold over her eyes kept her in the dark, and the gag stifled any moan or protest she might have made. She couldn't speak, couldn't see, could only feel—everything magnified, everything too intense. She was left alone with her thoughts and her body's treacherous reactions, unsure whether she should feel humiliated by the way she'd crumbled or surrender to the need building again within her.

The sheets pressed against the welts on her back, intensifying the ache in her skin, but beneath the pain was that lingering pleasure. She could feel the echo of her orgasm still pulsing through her, her body throbbing with a need she hadn't fully quenched. Every time she thought the sensations were fading, another ripple of pleasure would surge through her, her legs quaking as the overstimulation tipped her toward the edge again.

Leah's chest continued to rise and fall rapidly, her breath coming in shallow, desperate gasps as though the air around her had become scarce. The orgasm had left her drained, her body trembling in its aftermath, her lungs straining to fill themselves. Each ragged breath came out in stuttering wheezes as though her body was trying to recover from the relentless flood of sensations but couldn't quite manage it.

Her captor, watching her intently, seemed to savor the sight of her in this vulnerable, breathless state. He moved with deliberate slowness, his fingers grazing her damp skin as he began to loosen the gag from her mouth. The cloth slid away from her lips, releasing the pressure holding her voice captive. Her mouth opened slightly, but she made no sound, only gasping for the air she so desperately needed. The remnants of the gag left her jaw aching, but her body was too consumed by the struggle to breathe to register it fully.

The cool air of the room hit her damp lips, and for a moment, she thought she might finally catch her breath, but the residual tremors of her orgasm still coursed through her body, making her lungs falter. Her breathing remained ragged, like someone who had run a marathon but with no finish line in sight, no relief. Each inhale felt thin, insufficient, as though her chest couldn't expand enough to draw in the oxygen her body so badly needed.

At the same time, her captor reached for the blindfold. He pulled it away slowly as if to prolong the moment, the soft fabric slipping from her face. Leah blinked, her eyelids heavy, struggling to adjust to the dim light. The room was bathed in shadows, the faint glow from a nearby lamp barely illuminating the space. After so long in darkness, her eyes ached as they tried to make sense of the murky shapes around her.

Her vision was blurred as if the world had become a distorted version of itself. The low light only added to her disorientation, the shadows dancing on the edges of her perception. She blinked again, her lashes fluttering as her pupils dilated, trying to pull in more of the faint light. The room was hazy and unfamiliar, and though the blindfold was gone, a part of her still felt trapped in the darkness.

Her throat was dry, the words she might have spoken caught somewhere deep inside her, but the feeling of the gag's absence brought no immediate relief. Her captor loomed nearby, silent and watching, as if waiting for her to react, but she couldn't form any coherent thought. She felt dazed, her body still processing the overwhelming intensity of what had just happened. Every muscle was taut as if her body feared another touch, another sensation that might send her spiraling again.

She gasped softly, her struggle to breathe filling the room, punctuating the silence. The ache in her chest was palpable, her lungs burning from the effort, but no matter how hard she tried, she couldn't catch her breath fully. Her heart raced, thudding painfully in her ribcage, as if her body were stuck in a loop of arousal and exhaustion, neither entirely giving way to the other.

After what felt like an eternity, Leah's breaths began to steady, the rapid gasping giving way to something more controlled, though her body still hummed with residual tension. Her chest heaved one last time before the tightness in her lungs eased just enough for her to speak. She licked her dry lips, her voice hoarse and ragged as she struggled to find the strength to push the words past her throat.

"Blayne Alexander Guidry," she rasped, her tone of disbelief and anger punctuated by her breath's uneven rise and fall. "Just what the hell do you think you are doing?"

## Chapter 13

Blayne's eyes softened as he looked down at Leah, still bound and glistening with the sheen of her earlier release. "You looked like you were having trouble catching your breath," he said, his voice laced with concern despite the heat between them.

Leah released a shaky breath, her chest rising and falling as she worked to steady herself. "I was fine," she replied, her voice still slightly uneven as she tried to regain control. "And I hadn't even given you the signal that I was in distress."

Blayne's brow furrowed slightly, his gaze never leaving hers. "I've never seen you react that way during any of our role-playing sessions," he said, his memory of her trembling body still vivid. "I thought maybe you were struggling."

Leah exhaled deeply, her body finally settling into a more relaxed rhythm, though her heart still beat faster than usual. "I have to admit," she began, her voice dropping lower, "I've never had an orgasm that hit that hard in my life." She shifted slightly, feeling the dampness beneath her. A slow, teasing smile crept across her lips. "It was like... a whole other level. And judging by the wet spot I'm lying in, I'd say I've never been this turned on."

Blayne's lips curved into a faint grin as he glanced at the sheets. "I would have to agree," he said, his tone playful but tinged with awe. "I noticed the wet spot forming back when I started rubbing the feather across your body."

A shiver ran down Leah's spine at his words, her body involuntarily reacting to the memory. The feather... She could still feel the ghost of its touch, that delicate torment as it traced over her sensitive skin, teasing her until she thought she might break. "I have to admit," she said, her voice dropping to a sultry whisper, "I had trouble holding back an orgasm during that part of the session."

Blayne's grin widened, his eyes gleaming with satisfaction. "Well, I'm glad you enjoyed yourself."

"I did," Leah replied, her breath steadying as the earlier intensity gave way to something more playful. Her gaze locked onto his, and a mischievous smile tugged at her lips. "But you ended the session early... before you got to have any fun."

Blayne raised a brow, a flicker of surprise in his expression at the sudden shift in her tone. Leah's eyes glittered with mischief and desire, her body still humming from the aftermath of her release. "Now untie me," she continued, her voice soft but commanding, "so we can rectify that situation."

Blayne gave a low chuckle, his hand hovering over the knots that bound her wrists. The air between them was thick with unspoken promise, the connection between them reigniting as quickly as the fire had momentarily dimmed. He leaned down, his fingers grazing the knots as he slowly began to loosen them. His touch was deliberate, teasing even now as he freed her inch by inch, prolonging the moment.

Leah's pulse quickened again, her eyes fixed on his. Her body still ached with the memory of his touch, but there was something more now—a hunger that hadn't been sated, a desire that flared back to life the moment he came closer. Her wrists finally free, she rubbed them gently, her breath hitching in anticipation as she waited for what was to come.

Blayne stepped back, watching her with a mix of admiration and something darker, something more possessive. "Are you sure you're ready for this?" he asked, his voice low, his eyes never leaving hers.

Leah didn't hesitate. She pushed herself up, the wet sheets beneath her a reminder of just how far they had gone. "More than ready," she said with a sultry grin, her voice filled with confidence and desire. "Now it's your turn."

## Chapter 14

Leah worked at the Vermillion Parish Coroner's Office in Abbeville, Louisiana, where she was crucial in documenting and investigating every case that crossed the coroner's table. Anytime a body was found within the parish, Leah was one of the first to be called to assist. Her job was meticulous and often gruesome, requiring her to take detailed notes and photographs at crime scenes, ensuring that every detail was preserved for further analysis. Her camera captured the stark reality of death, and her notes recorded the clinical facts, but Leah had a way of distancing herself from the emotional weight of the scenes she witnessed.

Back in the lab, her responsibilities continued. She aided the coroner during autopsies, ensuring that every finding was logged carefully. She maintained precise documentation, cataloging everything from wounds and bruises to toxicology reports. It was often grim work, but Leah took pride in her attention to detail, knowing that her work could help bring justice for the victims and closure for their families. She was steady, calm, and professional, which are essential traits when working in such a sensitive and emotionally charged environment.

The day the first body was found was no different. Leah had received the call early in the morning and had gone out with the coroner to the scene deep in the bayous of Vermillion Parish. The woman had been found in a remote area, her body bound, gagged, and left to float among the cypress knees. The sight had been disturbing— this was no accident or random tragedy. It was something far darker.

Leah had taken the necessary photographs, capturing every angle, every detail, even as she felt a heavy sadness settle over her for the poor woman whose life had been so cruelly taken.

But as Leah documented the scene, another part of her mind wandered in ways she didn't fully understand. As she looked at the marks on her wrists and ankles, she felt a strange and conflicting sense of curiosity. She couldn't shake the thought that flashed through her mind—what would it be like to be in that position? To be bound, gagged, and blindfolded, entirely under someone else's control? The thought startled her, but she didn't push it away. Instead, it lingered, mixing with her sadness for the victim.

Blayne Guidry and Leah had been together for a few years before the first body was discovered. They had met at the annual Duck Festival, a festive occasion when Leah and Blayne first crossed paths. Their connection was immediate. Their relationship had been strong ever since, rooted in a shared love for their small towns and customs and enhanced by a playful side that carried into their private lives.

In the bedroom, Blayne and Leah had always enjoyed role-playing, a way to add excitement to their relationship. They trusted each other implicitly, and the dynamic they shared behind closed doors was a mix of fun, flirtation, and experimentation. It was a part of their relationship that they both found thrilling, and they never shied away from exploring new ideas together.

However, when the second body was found floating in the bayou, something shifted in Leah's mind. The details of the murders—women found bound, gagged, and stripped naked—had unsettled her, but not entirely in the way one might expect. While the town was gripped with fear over the gruesome nature of the killings, Leah found herself thinking about the dark fantasies she and Blayne had already dabbled in. The events unfolding in their community sparked a new idea in her, a role-playing scenario that blurred the lines between fantasy and reality.

By the time the third body surfaced, Leah had fully formed an elaborate plan for a night of role-play that mirrored the dreadful events in the town. She thought it was a way to spice things up between her and Blayne, using the adrenaline of the current situation to fuel the excitement. She meticulously crafted the scenario, knowing Blayne would go along with it because of the trust they had built over the years.

The plan was simple but detailed. After a night of fun and partying at the Duck Festival, Leah would pass out in the truck on the way home. This wasn't an unusual occurrence—she was a lightweight when it came to alcohol, and after a few drinks, she typically fell asleep quickly. Blayne would carry her into the house, as he'd done countless times before. But this time, when they got home, he would tie her up, blindfold her, and place a gag over her mouth—all part of the game they had prearranged.

Once she woke up, disoriented but safe under Blayne's watchful eye, he would play out the scenario they had discussed. He would cut off her clothes with a pair of scissors, the sound alone enough to send a thrill through her body. Then, as planned, he would introduce some light torture—a playful mix of restraint and teasing that would gradually build in intensity. It was all part of the game, something they both enjoyed: the delicate balance of control, pleasure, and anticipation.

Blayne was supposed to finish the night by ravishing her, taking the game to its natural conclusion. They had even discussed the finer details—he wouldn't finish inside her, mirroring the detail that had surfaced in the investigations about no semen being found on the bodies. It was meant to be a dark, thrilling experience, something wholly consensual and within the bounds of their relationship.

However, as the night unfolded, things didn't go as planned. Leah's breathing became heavier than usual, and her body reacted more intensely to the scenario than anticipated. The line between excitement and discomfort began to blur. Though fully immersed in the role-playing, Blayne became worried as Leah's breathing grew erratic. He wasn't sure if it was part of the act or if she was genuinely struggling. Concerned for her safety, he cut the scenario short.

Even though the murders remained an ongoing investigation, casting a dark shadow over the small, close-knit community, Blayne and Leah had shared a night they would never forget—though not for reasons anyone else could have guessed. In their secret world, it had been a night that brought their deepest fantasies to the surface, a twisted blend of excitement and fear that neither could shake.

That night, they had been attempting to push the boundaries of their relationship, to mix their mutual enjoyment of role play with the forbidden thrill that came from flirting with danger. Leah had meticulously crafted the plan, laying out every detail as though it were a performance they both were eager to enact. For them, it wasn't about recreating the horrors of the murders themselves but rather about exploring their shared fantasy of surrendering and taking control—of creating a world where, for a moment, they were able to play out the parts of captor and captive, bound by trust but tinged with the undeniable adrenaline of risk.

In their secret, sick, and twisted way, that night had brought them together, but it had also exposed the depths of their desires in a way that couldn't be undone. It was a night neither would ever forget—not because of the excitement, but because it had revealed something about them that now lingered beneath the surface of their relationship, forever shaping how they looked at each other and the world around them.

The End

Made in the USA
Columbia, SC
25 October 2024

44720993R00059